If Pete Was the Boy of Her Dreams, Why Did She Think so Much about Roger?

He always looked happy, and that was one of the things Karen admired about him. He was different, but he didn't seem to care.

"Do you write a lot of songs?" she asked him.

"Lately, no. But at other times, yes." Roger smiled. "Do you write songs, Karen?"

"Oh, no!"

"Poetry?"

Karen laughed at the thought. "No. I guess I'm just sort of ordinary."

He shook his head. "Never. None of us is ordinary, Karen. Each of us has a unique talent. Something special as our own gift."

For the first time it occurred to Karen that they might be friends—really good friends.

Dear Reader,

At Silhouette we publish books with you in mind. We're pleased to announce the creation of Silhouette First Love, a new line of contemporary romances written by the finest young-adult writers as well as outstanding new authors in this field.

Silhouette First Love captures many of the same elements enjoyed by Silhouette Romance readers—love stories, happy endings and the same attention to detail and description. But First Love features young heroines and heroes in contemporary and recognizable situations.

You play an important part in our future plans for First Love. We welcome any suggestions or comments on our books and I invite you to write to us at the address below.

Karen Solem
Editor-in-Chief
Silhouette Books
P.O. Box 769
New York, N.Y. 10019

PROMISED KISS
Veronica Ladd

First Love from Silhouette

Published by Silhouette Books New York

America's Publisher of Contemporary Romance

SILHOUETTE BOOKS, a Simon & Schuster Division of
GULF & WESTERN CORPORATION
1230 Avenue of the Americas, New York, N.Y. 10020

ISBN: 0-671-53314-2

First Silhouette Books printing February, 1982

10 9 8 7 6 5 4 3 2 1

For my dear friend,
loving sponsor, and
marvelous mentor
GENE FAIRLY

PROMISED KISS

1

Karen Williams straightened up, put her hands on her hips, and smiled at the warm May sun. She was happy to be working in her friend's garden, happy to be out of school, happy to be alive. A breeze pushed a lock of auburn hair from her forehead as birds sang from the flowering apple trees. She stretched her arms overhead, as though she were reaching for the sun, and said, "I love summer."

"Summer is fun," her friend Sue agreed. "At least, this summer is going to be fun. We won't be bored and lonely the way we are sometimes. You'll be running for queen and—"

"No." Karen interrupted softly. "I'm not going to be running for queen of the parade. I've made up my mind."

She laughed shortly and bent over to cut more

asparagus plants. Karen bent at the same time, swiftly cutting the slim green stalks at ground level. She worked easily, with clean, precise motions. It felt good to be moving in the warm sunlight, bending and stretching. She loved working in the soil, loved seeing green plants poke through the earth, then surge in growth. The asparagus plants always seemed like magic to her because they grew almost overnight.

She thought of telling Sue how she felt about the asparagus but decided not to. Though it was Sue's family garden they were working in, Karen was a much more devoted gardener. She'd been helping Sue for years. She and her mother and sister lived in a town apartment, so Karen helped Sue do her chores on Saturdays.

In a few minutes Sue straightened up and said, "That's enough. Let's go in and freeze these."

"But there are a lot more stalks that are ready," Karen protested.

"More we cut, the more we have to freeze," Sue said. Then she groaned in mock tiredness and said, "Time for a lemonade break."

"We just had lunch," Karen protested, but she followed her friend into the kitchen and rinsed the asparagus while Sue prepared the frozen lemonade.

They put the large kettle of water on the stove and sat down to enjoy the lemonade and cookies. When the water boiled, they would blanch the asparagus, put it in small plastic bags, and drop it in the large freezer on the back porch. Karen hoped that Sue's mother would come home and offer to send some of the asparagus home to Karen's house. It would be good to have asparagus for supper and it was too expensive to buy in the supermarket.

As Sue poured the pale yellow lemonade from the

orange plastic pitcher, Karen thought of canaries and daffodils. She held her cool glass in her hand and bit into a chocolate chip cookie. "I love yellow," she said. "It's the color of sunlight and flowers. It's my favorite color of all."

Sue nodded. "It's pretty, but your dress has to be pink. Pink will be best with your hair and eyes. Besides, your mother and sister wore pink dresses."

Karen sighed. The warm summer day suddenly seemed hot and sticky. She wished the chores were over and they could climb into Sue's car and whizz out to the lake or into town. She didn't want to work on a day like this. She wanted to be free, to run and run and run. . . .

"I'm not going to run for queen," Karen said again. This time she tried to make her voice sound firm and clear. "I don't want to be queen and I'm not going to run."

Sue chewed cookies and looked at her friend with interest for a minute. Then she shook her head and said, "That's silly. Of course you'll run. Ever since we were in second grade we've known you would be queen when we were sixteen."

"I know," Karen said. She could still remember the year her sister Lucy had been queen of the parade. She'd been seven then and she'd thought Lucy was the most beautiful girl in the whole world. Well, Lucy was still beautiful, but she was twenty-five years old and working at the bank. Lucy had changed and so had she. She tried to explain to Sue. "We were just kids. We didn't know how hard you have to work to be queen. We thought it was magic—like being Cinderella or something."

"It is magical," Sue insisted. "You'll love being queen once you get into it. Just imagine what it will be like standing up there on that float with those six handsome young men around you. Your dress will be pink and your flowers will be a deeper pink or maybe a deep red. American Beauty red is sort of purplish. Yes, American Beauty roses, and your hair will be long and shiny."

Karen laughed. "It's not going to be like that at all. In the first place, you have to get people to vote for you. That means you have to try and persuade people by going to church suppers and silly meetings and things all summer. You always have to be nice to everyone."

"But you're always nice anyway," Sue pointed out. She sounded as though she were finally hearing that Karen might be serious about not running for Queen of the Harvest Parade.

"The point is, you have to be a politician. I'm not. And besides, I think I would hate standing up there on that float having all the people stare at me. I'm really very shy."

"You shouldn't be," Sue said. "Besides, you know your mother and sister are counting on you. So forget that shy stuff. Let's get the asparagus finished."

Sue rose from the kitchen table and went to the sink. She started cutting the asparagus into smaller pieces so the pieces would fit into the plastic bags easily.

Karen did not rise from her chair to help Sue. Instead she sat with her elbows on the table, slumped over the cookie plate, and waited for a chance to bring the conversation back to the Harvest Parade. But Sue talked of other things as she worked. Sue's conversation was light and filled with small-town gossip of a sort that did not require much attention but made the work more interesting. It was obvious that she had no

intention of letting Karen return to her determination
not to run for queen.

Karen wanted to shout or cry or at least insist that
her friend stop chattering and pay some attention to
what she'd said. But Sue seemed to ignore Karen's
serious appearance. Finally, Karen stood up and said,
"I think I'll take a little walk."

"Walk?" Sue asked. "Where would you walk to?"

Karen laughed. "I'm going down to the edge of the
pasture. Maybe see the sheep. Maybe pick some wild
flowers to take home."

Sue shook her head. "You should be the one to live
out here in the sticks. I'd love to live in town."

Karen didn't point out to her friend that she lived in a
beautiful old rambling farmhouse while Karen lived in
a small, plain apartment. She was pretty sure that Sue
would hate sharing a bedroom with her sister, if she had
a sister, and she knew that Sue would hate having such
a small closet for her clothes.

Karen walked out of the kitchen, through the garden, and down the private road to the edge of the
pasture where the sheep were penned. As she walked,
some of her good mood returned. She could not help
but feel good on such a warm and wonderful day. The
sky was bright blue and small clouds scurried across the
horizon as though they were in a big hurry to get
somewhere else.

Softly, Karen began to sing an old song she'd learned
from her mother when she was a small child. "Blue
skies smiling at me. Nothing but blue skies do I see."
The breeze seemed absolutely perfect and Karen felt as
young and happy as the little lambs she saw trotting
along behind their mother. When she came closer to
the pasture fence, several sheep ran toward her, bleat-

ing a greeting. Though she knew they were hoping for food, not greeting her personally, Karen laughed aloud. Then she raised her voice and sang louder.

She leaned on the fence rail, singing to sheep, until Sue began honking the horn of her car. Karen glanced at her watch in surprise. It was almost three o'clock. She'd been out here singing to the sheep for more than an hour. She blushed at the thought, very glad that Sue hadn't come after her. It was this sort of absentminded dreaminess that made her friends and family think she was silly.

Karen speeded up, moving at a pace that was halfway between a run and a walk. Maybe it was silly to sing to sheep, but it had been fun. She began to try and think of something to answer Sue when her friend asked her what she'd been doing. She certainly wasn't crazy enough to admit to Sue that she'd been singing to the sheep. Sue hated sheep and never had anything to do with them at all.

But Sue didn't ask her what she'd been doing. Instead she teased, "Hey, Karen, how come you let me do all the work while you spend your time dreaming about Pete?"

Karen blushed as she usually did when anyone mentioned Pete Peterson by name. Sue glanced wryly at her friend as she pulled her car out of the driveway and onto the highway that led into town.

Sue said, "You know that Pete will be one of the guys on that queen's float, don't you?"

"Let's not talk about Pete," Karen begged.

"I love to talk about him," Sue teased. "I love to see you blush."

"I'm not blushing," Karen protested. "I have a sunburn."

"You never burn," Sue said. "It's one of the ways

14

that you're lucky. You've got that pretty peaches-and-cream skin and you just get a nice, darker peaches-and-cream color in the summer. You're blushing, not burning."

Karen felt uncomfortable, as she often did when her friend talked about her looks. She shifted in her seat and said, "I'm not as pretty as my sister Lucy."

"Probably not," Sue admitted. "But you are pretty, Karen. In fact, you're the prettiest girl in school. You've got deep auburn hair and great big gray eyes. You've got a straight nose and a heart-shaped face. You've even got a natural cupid's bow in your lips. And a dimple. And a good figure. And long fingernails. And—"

Karen broke into her friend's talk with a laugh. "You make me sound like a Barbie doll or something. I'm just an average-looking girl. You're pretty too."

"You just haven't realized it yet," Sue said. "But you're very, very pretty. And you'll be a beautiful queen."

"I'm not going to run for queen," Karen said. "Maybe you should run for queen, if you think it would be so great."

"I can't run for queen because I'm not popular enough," Sue said. "Or pretty enough," she added. "So you've got to do it. You've got to do it for me, for your mother, for your sister. For all of us," Sue added. Then she grinned. "And most of all, for Pete Peterson."

"Pete doesn't know I'm alive," Karen said.

"But he will if you run for queen," Sue said. "There's no way he'll be able to ignore you."

Karen sighed and looked out the car window at the countryside they were passing through. The trees and meadows seemed so bright and green now. Was it only a month or two ago that they had been bare? Even though she'd lived all sixteen years in Wilks, Kansas, Karen had never really gotten used to the surprise in the change of seasons. She said, "There are iris all along the roadside, Sue. Let's stop and pick some."

Sue groaned in mock despair and said, "Okay, nature girl. You can pick them. I'll give you three minutes."

When the car stopped, Karen got out and picked half a dozen of the wild iris. She cradled them in her arms as she came back to the car. Looking down at the soft, velvety purple with deep centers, she thought of butterfly wings and dusk at the lake. She held the flowers close and smiled happily. "I love summer," she repeated. "Everything is so lovely."

"And this will be the best summer of all," Sue promised. "You'll see. You'll have a date with Pete by the Fourth of July. Best of all, at Labor Day, you'll be queen of the county."

"And you?" Karen asked. "What will you be doing?" She often felt guilty because her friend seemed so much more interested in her activities and happiness than her own. "What will your summer be like?"

Sue looked a little surprised as she answered. "I already have a boyfriend and I'll be your campaign manager. It will be fun—you'll see."

Karen buried her head in the wild iris, trying not to get depressed by her friend's expectations of her. Sue was going to really be disappointed when she found out that Karen was serious about not running for queen. Karen closed her eyes and bent closer to the flowers. Sue wasn't the only one who was going to be disappointed. Her mother and sister would be heartbroken when she told them.

As she thought of her mother, tears came to her eyes.

Her mother worked so hard and was such a nice woman. Her mother was sure that being queen would make Karen happy the way it had made her happy twenty-seven years ago. It had also made her sister Lucy happy nine years ago. But Karen was sure that being queen of the parade would never make her happy.

Maybe it would be easier to run than to tell them, Karen thought, as she had thought many times before. She sighed a deep sigh and closed her eyes tighter. No matter what she chose to do, she would be in trouble. It was going to be hard to convince her mother and sister she didn't want to run. It would be even harder to convince other people to vote for her.

It isn't just that I'm shy, Karen told herself. She knew that it was hard for Sue or Lucy or her mother to imagine that any girl wouldn't be happy standing up on that float, having been chosen Queen of Wilks County. But Karen was sure it would only make her miserable. She hated being the center of attention, even when it was favorable attention. It just wasn't for her.

The only reason she was even remotely interested in being queen was that Pete Peterson would be one of the escorts. Ever since Karen had been a very young girl, she'd had a crush on Pete. So had a lot of other girls in Wilks County, and Karen knew he wasn't interested in her at all. If she thought that being queen would really get her a date with Pete, she might be interested enough to go through the struggle of trying to win the contest. But Pete could have his pick of all the girls around. Why would he be interested in her? No, she promised herself. No. I won't run for queen, and that's definite.

"You're talking to yourself," Sue teased as she swung the car to a halt.

Karen opened her eyes abruptly. "Where are we?" she asked. But Sue didn't need to answer. They were in the Peterson gas station and Pete Peterson was walking toward Sue's car.

"Oh, no," Karen protested to her friend. "You promised you wouldn't do this again."

"Good for you," Sue said. "You've got to get over that shyness somehow. Now don't blush."

Karen could already feel her cheeks flaming as she dropped her head to keep from looking at Pete. She was so embarrassed and she was sure he would know that Sue had come there just to see him. But even a loyal friend like Sue should know it was hopeless. Pete would never notice her. She was too shy to even look at him. What would he want with a girl like her?

2

She heard his voice saying, "Hi, Karen." It was a nice voice, with a warm, deep tone.

Karen lifted her head and looked directly into Pete Peterson's eyes. He was tall, blond, and very handsome with wide cheekbones and dark blue eyes. His eyebrows were much darker than his hair and they arched above his eyes, giving him a dramatic look. Of course, Karen had known Pete all her life, and she knew that he was a very nice person. That was part of the reason she was attracted to him.

She was only one of a large group of girls who were interested in Pete. The funny thing was that he was nice to everyone, but he didn't seem to be particularly interested in anyone. Now Karen tried to keep her own voice even and calm as she answered, "Hi, Pete. How are you?"

"Fine. How about you?"

"Fine."

Pete sort of leaned against the car, looking directly at Karen. He cleared his throat and asked, "You've been fine?"

"Fine." Karen hoped that Sue wouldn't laugh or say something sharp about how silly her conversation was. But for once Sue was quiet.

The silence seemed very long. The gas hose clicked off and the meter rang. Karen managed to say, "I think the gas thing shut off."

Pete looked surprised. "Yes. Well, ah . . . would you like to go for a Coke or something?"

Karen was afraid her voice would close up on her. "Aren't you working?"

"No. I mean, I saw it was you so I waited on you, but I'm finished. Want to go somewhere?"

"Go ahead," Sue answered quickly.

Karen supposed that her friend was afraid she'd be so shy she wouldn't answer correctly. Nevertheless, it bothered her to have her friend answer for her. She said, "I'd like that."

"Good," Pete said, and opened the door.

Karen realized that both Sue and Pete expected her to get out of Sue's car and follow Pete over to his car, which was parked beside the station building. She didn't feel right about that, but there wasn't really anything else to do. She turned to Sue and asked, "Won't you come too?"

Sue frowned at her in warning and shook her head. "You have a good time." Then Sue handed Pete money for the gas and sped away.

Karen felt really peculiar standing on the asphalt pavement waiting for Pete to wash up. She was nervous and irritable, somehow blaming Sue for getting her into this awkward situation. She wished that she'd refused Pete and suggested that he call her at home. Hopping out of Sue's car to go with Pete seemed undignified and somehow crude. But she told herself all that was silly and tried to look cheerful as Pete walked toward her. Her heart was thumping so loudly that she was sure he would be able to hear it. Or, if not that, he would know how terrified she was by the way her voice sounded. There was a lump in her throat so large that she was sure everything was going to come out a croak.

Get a grip on yourself, she admonished herself. She was very frightened that she would do something or say something so awful that Pete would never be interested in her again. If, after all these years of yearning for him, she should ruin everything by stupidity, she'd never forgive herself. Even as she was thinking all these thoughts, she was telling herself that this was her dream come true. Pete had asked her out! It had finally happened! And even if he never noticed her again, she would have this one time. This was better than anything that had ever happened to her before.

It was a bright, sunny day and the sun was behind Pete. As he walked toward her, his golden hair shone like a halo. Karen had to turn her eyes away because she was looking straight into the sun and she didn't want to squint. She wished she were comfortable in dark glasses because she always admired them on other girls. They looked so sophisticated and Karen knew she could stand some extra sophistication. But dark glasses were always slipping down her nose or she would leave them behind and never recover them. She sighed. She would just never be the sophisticated type.

Pete was beside her now, looking down at her with a smile and asking, "Want to go to the lake for a hamburger?"

"I'll have to call home," Karen answered quickly. She was surprised and pleased that he was apparently expecting to spend a part of the evening with her, not just taking her out for a Coke, as he'd proposed earlier. She hoped he wouldn't think it was silly or childish for her to ask permission from her mother. She tried to explain, "I'm sure it will be all right. But my mother would worry."

"Sure," Pete said. "You can use the phone in the station."

As he talked to her, he bent his head forward slightly, as though he wanted to be closer to her. Karen couldn't get over the fact that Pete was actually standing there talking to her as though she were someone special. Of course, she'd talked to Pete before. You couldn't live in a small town like Wilks and not know everyone. But she and Pete probably hadn't really said more than three words to each other in the last three years. In fact, Karen was pretty sure the last time Pete had said anything to her directly, it had been in the sixth grade. They'd both been shepherds in the Christmas play and Pete had accused her of stepping on the back of his robe.

Now he asked, "You need a dime to call?"

Karen reached in her Levis pocket and pulled out a small coin purse. She looked quickly, saw that she had two dimes and a dollar bill, and shook her head. Then she ran lightly to the gas station building, hoping that Pete wouldn't be too critical of the way she was dressed. After all, if he'd given her any notice, she could have changed into her white slacks and yellow T-shirt. But since this was a spur-of-the-moment date, he would have to settle for the old orange shirt and faded Levis she was wearing.

Her mother wasn't home from the bakery yet, but

her sister Lucy said she should go and have a good time. Karen said, "Thanks, Lucy—I know it's my night to cook. But I'll do something nice for you sometime."

"Sure, Hon," Lucy said. Then she added, "If I ever get a date again."

Karen walked more slowly back to Pete, thinking for a moment about her sister Lucy's last little bitter joke. Though she was the most beautiful unmarried woman in town, it was true that Lucy wasn't dating much lately. Karen wondered why. Was it because she'd turned so many guys down that they'd decided she was not going to marry at all? Or was it because Lucy was at the age where most of her friends were married? Was Lucy becoming an old maid? Karen had to laugh at the old-fashioned idea. No one worried about things like that anymore—did they?

"What's the joke?" Pete asked as she came back to him. "Are you laughing at my girl friend?"

"Girl friend?" Karen asked in a puzzled voice.

"My cute little Sally over there." Pete pointed to his car. It was a small Volkswagen Beetle with bright yellow doors and a black body. Karen had seen the car many times before so she shook her head. "No, I've seen you in it for a year now. Though this is the first time you've ever offered me a ride."

"Is it?" Pete looked surprised. "Well, it's about time you got acquainted with Sally. She's my best girl." Then he grinned and added, "So far. It may be time to make some changes in my life."

Karen wished with all her heart that she had a quick answer to Pete's light banter. But she was still surprised to be asked out at all. Being with Pete seemed to make her more tongue-tied and unsure of herself than she had ever been. She tried to tell herself that it was silly. After all, she'd known Pete since kindergarten. They lived on the same side of town and had always been in the same school, though Pete was a year ahead of her. But though she'd known Pete forever, she'd had a crush on him forever also. It didn't help her with fast and light conversation to think of the many times she'd hoped that he'd notice her.

Karen smiled and opened the car door. As she climbed inside the small black and yellow Beetle, she said, "Yellow is my favorite color."

Pete was beside her now, starting the motor and slipping the Volkswagen out onto the street. He said, "My favorite color is blue, like your eyes."

Karen couldn't help but laugh. "My eyes are gray."

Pete laughed louder and said sheepishly, "Serves me right to try such a corny old line on a nice girl like you, Karen."

As Pete spoke her name, Karen shivered lightly. How many times had she dreamed of having Pete speak her name like that? How many times had she hoped that he would ask her out for a Coke, for a ride in the country, to a dance—anything at all. And here she was beside him, zooming out of town toward the lake!

She glanced sideways at his profile. His eyes were blue as the deepest water on the lake. His nose was straight and perfect. She remembered how frightened she'd been last year during the first football game of the season. Pete had been hurt and she'd sat in the stands, holding her breath until they announced that he was all right. She asked, "Will you play football again this year?"

Pete nodded. "I should be better at it. But who cares about football? Who cares about anything at all but summer? We've got a whole summer before school starts again. Course, I'll have to work. Guess you'll be busy too."

"I don't have a job," Karen said. "I thought I might try and fill in at the bakery where my mother works when people go on vacation."

"But you'll be running for queen. Running for queen is a big deal."

Karen felt her heart begin to beat more quickly. Did she dare tell Pete she wasn't going to run? Was the reason he'd suddenly asked her out because she might be Harvest Queen? She said slowly, cautiously, "I think each year it gets a bit more complicated to win. When my sister ran, all she had to do was get a sponsor and go to a few Grange meetings. Apparently when my mother won, the Lions Club just put her picture in the paper."

"Yeah," Pete said. "But the girl who ran from the Lions Club last year actually went door to door to campaign."

Karen felt a sharp stab of fear in her stomach. She said, "I would hate that."

Pete laughed and patted her hand. "You'll be good at it once you start. What organization is sponsoring you?"

Now was the time to tell him the truth. Now was the time to tell Pete that she wouldn't be running for queen at all. Now was the time to find out whether or not Pete's interest in her was because he thought she was running for queen. Now was the time . . . No! Karen thought. I won't tell him yet. She told herself that she would let this one date be just as perfect as it could be. She would tell him tomorrow if she saw him, but this night was special.

"I don't know," she answered. That was true enough, as far as it went. "But let's talk about something else. I don't want to think about the contest right now."

Pete looked at her quickly and she realized that he must have heard the note of desperation in her voice. She blushed again and wished that she were not so self-conscious around him. Why did she have to be so shy? Why couldn't she just enjoy the dream come true?

They went to Jack's At The Beach for hamburgers and Cokes. It was a run-down old restaurant with a fancy name, but it was very popular with teenagers in Wilks County. Karen saw a lot of people she knew and she was pleased that she was with Pete. It felt good to be out with one of the most popular boys in school. She could tell by the way the kids said hello that they were impressed.

They ate hamburgers and talked; then they played the jukebox and danced for a while. By eight o'clock, it was almost dark outside and Pete suggested they take a walk around the lake.

As they walked, Pete held Karen's hand and talked about school and his job at the gas station. It was an easy conversation and Karen tried to relax and enjoy being with him. She tried to add the right comments at the right time because she wanted to appear interested in Pete's life, but at the same time she didn't want to appear overeager. She was very conscious that her hand was in his.

Karen had dated several other boys during the last two years, but she'd never been this nervous. She tried to remind herself that she'd never dated a boy who was as popular or as good-looking as Pete. She tried to remind herself that Pete was the same kid she'd known when she was in grade school. But even then, she'd looked up to Pete and thought he was a very, very special person. And since sixth grade she'd dreamed of a night like this.

In junior high school, she'd wiled her way through

dull classes by trying to draw Pete's picture on the edges of her notebook paper. Somehow she'd never been able to get his face exactly right. Now she glanced up quickly at Pete, looking at his nose in profile. Yes, it was as straight as she'd thought. But why was it that in her drawings she'd never been able to capture that easy smile? Or those nice, round blue eyes?

The sun was almost down now and the lake sounds were changing. Most of the motorboats pulled into shore and the insects began to sing louder than before. Suddenly, the lake seemed a very romantic place to be. Funny how something you've seen all your life can take on a different mood when you're with the right person, Karen thought.

Pete said it out loud. "You know, I've been here lots of times, but tonight seems different. More . . . nicer." He turned to her and put his arm around her shoulder, pulling her close to him. He kissed her on the lips, holding her very tight, and for a moment Karen wanted to turn and run. Then she whispered to herself that this was what she'd dreamed of.

Somewhere a radio was playing and people were laughing. Somewhere there were sounds of a motorboat and people talking. Somewhere a dog was barking and insects were singing. All the distant sounds blended into soft summer evening music. As Karen responded to Pete's kiss, she thought, This is a night to remember. This is my special night.

They walked a bit farther along the shore of the lake. Karen shivered. Pete put his arm around her shoulder. "Cold?"

"A little," Karen admitted. Then she added, "I think it's about time for me to go home." It was almost ten o'clock. Karen knew that Pete had a lot of girls chasing him. She didn't want to be one of those girls who pushed too hard. Even though she was having a good time, she was sure it was time to go home. After all, he'd invited her for a Coke and they'd spent five hours together.

Pete didn't argue with her. He took her straight home, kissed her good night, and said, "It was a great evening, Karen."

"Yes," Karen agreed. She was hoping with all her heart that he would ask her out again. When he said nothing else, she smiled at him and slipped inside the entrance door of her apartment building.

Once inside, Karen leaned against the door and tried to sort out her emotions. On the one hand, she was so very happy that Pete had finally noticed her. On the other hand, she was disappointed that he hadn't asked for another date. One minute she was elated with joy, when she thought about their kisses, and the next minute she was ready to cry because he hadn't been interested enough to suggest they get together again. On top of all her other hopes and fears, she couldn't help wondering how much of his newfound interest in her was because of the parade coming up.

Despite her confused feelings, Karen fell asleep very quickly. She was still sleeping at ten o'clock in the morning when Sue called. Her friend's first question was, "Did he ask you out again?"

"No," Karen admitted. Then she added quickly, "But I had a good time."

"Of course you had a good time," Sue said. "You've been waiting for him to ask you out for years."

Karen couldn't think of anything else to say to her friend. There was a long pause on the telephone and Karen felt very uncomfortable. Finally, she asked, "What are you going to do today?"

"I'm supposed to meet John for a Coke around six. He works till then," Sue answered.

Sue's boyfriend, John Wiggens, worked for his uncle in a hardware store in a neighboring small town. Though Sue complained because John wasn't more available, Karen sometimes wondered if that was really the way Sue felt. They'd been going together for two years now, and Karen had the feeling at times that Sue was bored by John. He was a nice person but never had much to say.

"We could go to the lake after church," Karen suggested.

"Good idea," Sue said quickly. "We might run into Pete. Don't give up hope."

"I haven't given up hope," Karen said with a slight edge to her voice. Karen wanted to tell Sue that Pete had at least been interested enough in her to kiss her, but she didn't. Somehow Sue's attitude made her feel like keeping that secret.

Sue picked up Karen right on time and the two girls drove out to the lake. As they passed the small white houses on the side streets of town, Karen watched the picket fences and flower gardens. Occasionally she would point out a particularly lovely yard, but Sue wasn't really interested. Sue talked most of the way to the lake about the television show she'd seen earlier that week. Karen was grateful that her friend's subject was television rather than her date with Pete or the Harvest Parade.

The lake wasn't far from town, but Karen always felt as though she were in a different part of the world when the car pulled up to the gravel parking lot. There were willow trees and small bushes almost up to the edge of the water. The lake was only about a mile wide at the widest point, but it seemed to be the loveliest spot in the world this afternoon.

The willow trees seemed to be a bright green instead of the usual blue-green color, the water was a bright aqua, and everywhere Karen looked the sun was making things sparkle. Even though there were quite a few cars parked in the lot, the main part of the lake was empty of boats. Most of the people would be swimmers today and all of the swimming was confined to one small section of the lake. That was fine with Karen because she loved looking out over the empty blue water. It always gave her a feeling of peace and happiness to be in this beautiful natural setting.

There were a lot of kids at the lake that afternoon, but Pete wasn't one of them. Karen and Sue chose a spot not too far from the restaurant where Karen had eaten with Pete last night. As they spread their towels out on the warm sand, Karen said, "I love the summer. Think I'll go swimming."

"Don't go swimming!" Sue said. "What if Pete comes along? Your hair will be all wet."

Karen dropped down on the towel and rolled on her stomach to try to get a tan on her back. She closed her eyes and let the warm sunshine play on her skin. Soon, beads of perspiration began to form around the edges of her bathing suit. She felt hot and sticky. She thought of the fresh cool water just waiting for her.

Finally, she could stand it no longer. She rolled over, sat up, pulled up the straps of her two-piece bathing suit and said, "I'm going in. Want to come?"

"You're crazy," Sue warned. "How do you know Pete won't show up?"

Karen stood up, said, "If Pete comes around, I'll tell him I'm a mermaid or something. Coming?"

Sue shook her head no and turned away. Soon Karen was splashing into the cold, clear water. It felt almost painfully cold because she'd been so hot when she was on shore, but she was soon enjoying herself.

She swam directly out to the center of the lake, loving the feel of her body cutting through the water, loving the feel of using her muscles. She was a good swimmer and she moved in the water with ease. She started swimming in circles, diving and coming to the surface, arching her back like a porpoise. She was having a wonderful time, totally oblivious to the world around her. Finally, she was tired enough to turn around and swim toward shore.

She was breathing slightly harder than normal as she swam by the large wooden floating dock that was anchored about fifty feet offshore. When she heard someone call her name, she swam toward the float to see who it was.

Roger Micklovich waved his arm and called out, "Come on up."

Karen was slightly disappointed that it wasn't Pete. She wasn't surprised to see that Roger was on the dock all alone though. Roger was alone a lot, at least partly because he was new in town. But Karen also suspected that Roger didn't mind being alone as much as most people did.

She changed her course slightly and swam over to the floating dock. Roger reached over the edge and held out his hand. He said, "Here, I'll help you."

Karen laughed and shook her head. "I can manage." She grabbed hold of the sides of the wooden dock and pulled herself up in the water. Then she swung one of her long legs over the edge and climbed onto the dock. She asked, "What are you doing out here all alone?"

"Thinking," Roger said. "Actually, I was trying to write lyrics for a song. But mostly I was thinking."

"You write songs?" Karen asked. She wasn't sure how she felt about that. It seemed like kind of an odd thing to do. But Roger was different in a lot of ways. He was taller than Pete, but he didn't play football. In fact, he didn't play any sports. He was always friendly, but he spent a lot of time alone. What was more, he didn't seem to mind it. Roger always looked happy and that was one of the things that Karen admired about him. He was different, but he didn't seem to care. It seemed like everyone else she knew cared a lot about being just like everyone else—only better.

As she sat down beside Roger, pulling her long wet legs up under her chin, she was surprised at how much she'd thought about Roger. He'd been in town a few months, but she'd never really talked to him and she wasn't sure what to say. "What kind of songs?" she asked.

Roger pointed at the one lonely cloud in the sky and answered, "Songs like this: 'Lone cloud, swing soft/ Lone cloud, love long/Lone cloud, fly aloft/Lone cloud, hear my song.'" Then he made a face and said, "Bad songs, I guess. At least that one is bad. I guess all this fresh air and sunshine is making my brain soft."

"You're from the city, aren't you?" Karen asked suddenly. "What's it like?"

"Chicago? It's big and crowded and noisy. This is nicer—at least in most ways."

Karen thought she heard a slight note of homesickness in his voice. She asked softly, "Is it hard to come to a new town? Hard to make friends?"

"Sometimes," Roger admitted.

Karen wanted to ask him why he'd moved to Wilks, but she felt it would be prying. Somehow she thought of Roger as belonging in a big city—not a small county township like this one. She didn't know Roger well enough to ask him about his personal life, so she asked instead, "Do you write a lot of songs?"

"Lately, no. But at other times yes." Roger smiled and asked her, "Do you write songs?"

"Oh, no!"

"Poetry?"

Karen laughed at the thought. "No. Nothing."

Roger said softly, "That's funny. I had you pegged as a girl who wrote poetry or at least read a lot of it."

"Never," Karen said. Then she added, "I guess I'm just sort of ordinary."

He shook his head and said, "Never. None of us is ordinary, Karen. Each of us has a unique talent. Something special as our special gift."

Karen looked at him for a minute. Was he kidding? She really didn't know what to think about a fellow who talked like that. She knew he was different. She also knew he was smart, but even Alan Riddings, who got straight A's in school, didn't talk like that. And no one she knew read poetry unless the teacher assigned it. Finally she decided that Roger wasn't kidding. His clear gray eyes were too open and serious to be making fun of her. She said, "I don't have a gift. At least, I don't know what my gift is, if I have one."

"Then you'll have fun learning," Roger said. He was smiling now and Karen realized that he wasn't really bad-looking at all. He had a nice smile and nice eyes. His hair was very curly and he wore it longer than any of the other boys in town, but it was nice hair. Karen wondered what it was about Roger that made the other kids think he was so weird. She decided she liked him even if he did read poetry and talk about different things.

"Swimming is one of your gifts," Roger said suddenly. "I was watching you out there. Like a selkie, you were."

"Selkie?" Karen asked.

"A magical sea creature. Half human, half seal," Roger explained. "There's lots of songs and stories about them. Haven't you heard them?"

"No," Karen said quickly. But Roger's mention of sea creatures had reminded her of her own mention of mermaids earlier that afternoon. Sue would be worried about her by now. She'd been gone too long. She told Roger that she had to get back and dove into the water to swim to shore.

When she got back to Sue, she explained, "I ran into Roger Micklovich on the floating dock."

"That creep," Sue said.

"He's not a creep," Karen protested. "I like him."

A few minutes later, Roger came over to their spot on the beach. He smiled and said, "Hi, Sue. Hi, Karen."

"Hi, Roger," Karen answered, returning his smile.

"Mind if I join you?" he asked.

Karen was afraid that Sue would say something to hurt his feelings, so she said very quickly, "Of course not, Roger. Drop your towel right here."

Sue glared at her and rolled over on her stomach so that she wouldn't have to look at Roger. Karen knew that she would get a lecture from her friend when he left, but she didn't care. Roger was a nice guy and she didn't want to hurt him. So no matter what Sue thought, she was going to be nice to him.

They talked awhile about nothing in particular. Sue continued to ignore them and Karen felt a little awkward about the whole situation. She didn't want to be too nice to Roger because she certainly didn't want to encourage him. She would feel awful if he called her for a date or anything like that.

She found herself thinking about her date with Pete last night. Why hadn't he asked her out again? Had she done something wrong? Maybe she appeared too eager or too shy for him. Karen wanted so much to have Pete like her now she was sure that she hadn't succeeded in making a good impression on him.

"I guess I'll run along now," Roger said.

Suddenly Karen realized that she'd been so busy thinking about Pete she'd forgotten that Roger was there talking to her. She hadn't heard a word he'd said for at least five minutes. And he knew it. That was why he was leaving now.

"Okay," she said because she didn't know what else to say. "It was fun talking to you."

"I'll sing you that song sometime," he said.

"Song?"

"The selkie song, the one I was telling you about," he answered softly. His gray eyes met hers for an instant.

Before he was out of hearing distance, Sue said, "You shouldn't talk to a creep like that. It will ruin your chances if you hang out with unpopular weirdos like that."

"Chances?" Karen asked.

"Your chances with Pete," Sue explained. "And your chances to be queen of the parade."

A tired sadness washed over Karen. How was she ever going to find the right words to explain it to Sue? How could she even hope to convince her friend that she really didn't want to be voted the queen when she didn't understand it very well herself? Maybe Sue was right. Maybe she was just shy. Or maybe she was some kind of weirdo herself. Maybe she hadn't talked to Roger to be nice but because they were alike.

Karen sat up and said quietly, "I am not going to run for queen. As for Pete, I don't think I have a chance with him anyway. Now let's go home before we're both red as lobsters."

Sue looked as though she wanted to say a lot more but she didn't mention Roger, the parade, or Pete again that day. Perhaps, thought Karen, she thinks I'm going to change my mind. Or perhaps she suspects how upset I really am. Sue and I have been friends a long time. Maybe she knows me. Maybe she knows how close to tears I am right this minute. Maybe.

3

Karen was home in time to cook supper for Lucy and her mother. She tried to break her sad mood by paying special attention to the menu. As she chopped the vegetables for the Chinese dish she was preparing, she rehearsed what she would say to Lucy and her mother tonight. She had to find better words to explain to them why she didn't want to run for queen. She obviously hadn't been able to explain it very well to Sue.

Her mother looked tired and Lucy had a date, so Karen said, "I'll do the dishes."

"It's my night," Lucy said. "I have time. My date won't pick me up till eight thirty."

"You did them for me last night," Karen reminded her.

Lucy smiled gratefully and said, "Okay. How was your date anyway?"

"Fine," Karen said. Then she took a deep breath and began her rehearsed speech. "I think you'll be disappointed, but I know you'll understand. I've definitely decided not to run for Queen of the Harvest Parade."

"But this is your year!" Her mother said in alarm. "It is only open to sixteen- and seventeen-year-olds. By next summer you'll be too old."

"Not a good idea to wait till next year," her sister chimed in. "Once you graduate from high school, people will think of you as out of the running. Besides, everyone expects you to be this year's queen."

"In the first place," Karen said, "it isn't fair to make the girls run for queen and appoint the boys as escorts. Why don't they make the boys run too?"

"You know the answer to questions like that! It's always been done that way. It's the way it was done when I was a girl and it's the way it's done now," said her mother crossly.

"Besides, they have six boys and only one girl," Karen went on. "That's not fair either."

"You're just complaining about the rules because you're shy," Lucy said. "You think it will be hard to be up on that float having everyone look at you. But you'll see—"

"It's wonderful," her mother broke in. As it usually did when Mrs. Williams talked about the Harvest Parade, her face took on a softer, younger look.

Karen felt tears start in her eyes. Her mother, who was only forty-three years old, looked like an old and tired woman. It was hard to imagine that she'd ever been as young and pretty as Lucy. Her feet were swollen from standing on them all day, and Karen noticed that a few varicose veins were beginning to break out on her ankles. Karen's feelings moved back and forth between sadness and frustration. Her mother seemed to go over the same old things all the time. She seemed to repeat herself so much. It was hard not to be impatient with her.

Sitting on the wooden kitchen chair, sipping her coffee, Marsha Williams described the dress she wore as Harvest Queen. "There were ruffles on the skirt, small nylon ruffles that were held together with small pink flowers. And the ruffles got bigger and bigger as they came toward the ground. You know what I mean—the ones up near my waist were teeny . . ." Here she held up two fingers to show the width of the ruffles. Both her daughters pretended to look with interest, though they'd both heard every word of this many times before.

". . . and the skirt was so full. It took seven petticoats to fill it out. Those were the days of stiff petticoats, at least on formals."

Instead of letting her mother continue with the description of the gown, as she usually would, Karen interrupted. "Weren't you hot?" she asked. "Labor Day is always hot and with that kind of a heavy dress—"

Her mother looked surprised at the thought, though she complained all the time about the simple nylon uniforms she wore at the bakery. "Hot? I don't remember. All I remember was those handsome boys and the flowers and the people. It was the happiest day of my life." Marsha Williams sighed heavily. Then she obviously forced herself to add, "Except for when my girls were born. Those were the happiest days of all. For every woman."

Privately Karen wondered how happy her mother could have been. Two children and then a divorce were a lot for any woman to handle. And before Lucy went to work in the bank, times had been hard. Things were easier now. They even had a little money that Aunt Alice had left to each of them. Her mother had had a hard life, Karen thought. It was no wonder that being Harvest Queen seemed so wonderful to her. But my life won't be like that, Karen promised herself. And even as she made herself the promise, she felt a tiny knot of fear in her heart. Weren't most people's lives like that?

"I know being Harvest Queen was wonderful for you," Karen said gently. "But I wouldn't like it. You're . . . you're more extroverted than I am. You love to laugh and joke with people at the bakery. You have lots of friends. I'm shy."

"You're not very shy," her mother said quickly. She never liked to hear anything bad about her two wonderful, beautiful girls, as she called Karen and Lucy. "No. You're very popular and pretty. Everyone likes you."

Karen turned from her mother to her sister. Sometimes Lucy, who was closer to her own age, could help her explain things to her mother. But Lucy dropped her eyes and didn't answer Karen's unspoken plea. Karen tried again. This time she said, "Mother, when you ran for Harvest Queen, all you had to do was put your picture in the paper. You were chosen because everyone knew you and liked you—"

"And that's why you'll be chosen," her mother broke in.

"But now they expect you to campaign," Karen said. There was that note of desperation in her voice again. "Even when Lucy ran, all she had to do was go to some suppers and stuff. But last year the girl who won went door to door."

"I wouldn't want you to do that unless you took Sue or another girl friend with you," her mother said. "It wouldn't look nice."

"I don't want to go door to door!" Karen wailed. She was close to tears now. Talking to her mother was as hopeless as talking to Sue.

"Don't yell at Mama," Lucy said quickly. "No one wants to force you. We just want you to be happy. Any girl would love to be Harvest Queen, and you have a chance."

"That's another thing," Karen said. "Why is everyone so sure that I'll win? There are other girls running."

"You'll win," Lucy said. Her voice sounded so definite that Karen knew she really believed that.

"Of course you'll win," her mother chimed in. "I won and Lucy won, so you can win too."

Karen felt the tears rise to her eyes. It was absolutely hopeless to try and explain things to them. They just wouldn't listen to her. No one cared about her at all. They just wanted the glory for themselves. No—she corrected herself quickly—her mother and sister really loved her. It was just that they honestly couldn't imagine that she didn't want to be Harvest Queen. In their eyes no girl in her right mind would turn down a chance like this.

"I'm not going to do it," Karen said.

Her mother stood up, put her hands on Karen's shoulder, and said, "Of course you'll do it. You'll see. When you get into that mood, you don't think straight. But there's nothing more wonderful than being Harvest Queen, is there, Lucy?"

"No," Lucy said. She too stood up, stretching her arms overhead and bending to touch her toes. "Just thinking about it makes me feel young and pretty again."

"What foolishness," her mother laughed. "Karen thinks she is too shy and you think you're getting old. Anyone knows that my two girls are the prettiest, nicest, and best girls in Wilks County."

Karen and Lucy exchanged looks. Lucy kissed her mother on the cheek and said, "Okay, Mama Tiger, we're perfect. And that makes you perfect too. Right?"

For the first time that evening Marsha Williams's face relaxed. "Right," she agreed with a mock fierceness.

Karen smiled at her mother and said, "Of course you're perfect and you were a beautiful Harvest Queen and you're still beautiful."

"Your sister was more beautiful," her mother said quickly. "And you'll be the most beautiful of all."

Karen laughed at the idea. She said, "Everyone knows that Lucy is the Fairest in the Land. No, I won't outshine my sister or my mother. But I'll do my best."

Lucy looked at her quickly, as though she wanted to question Karen's sudden capitulation, but all she said was, "Fairest in the Land or not, Prince Charming will be angry if I keep his coach waiting."

"Who's the Prince Charming tonight?" Karen asked.

Lucy laughed. "It's Jim Arnold. I guess he's not exactly an answer to my dreams, but he's sweet and *single.*"

"Sweet and single," Karen teased. "That sounds like the lyrics to a song." Suddenly, Karen thought of Roger Micklovich and she wondered what he would think about her running for queen. She already knew that her mother and sister and Sue and probably Pete, if he knew, thought she was crazy to even hesitate. Now she was so far from normal that she was looking for help from a creep like Roger. What's wrong with me? she asked herself. Why am I so different?

4

In a way, Karen felt better after she gave up and said she would run for queen of the parade. It seemed to make everyone else so happy. Now that she'd decided that she would run, she tried to tell herself that it was going to be as much fun as Sue and Lucy and her mother promised.

She did manage to sound enthusiastic when her mother said that the Lions Club had agreed to sponsor her, just as they'd sponsored her sister and mother. "They're the biggest organization," Marsha Williams said. "I was afraid that they'd want to sponsor Charlotte Melville because she's Larry Melville's niece and Larry is so active in the Lions. But Tom Whitaker dropped by today to tell me to tell you to pick up your letter tomorrow."

"That's wonderful," Karen said. Her mother's voice

and manner seemed so happy that Karen did find herself thinking it was wonderful for a moment. Then she asked, "Who will sponsor Charlotte?"

"Oh, she'll get someone," Marsha Williams answered.

Karen smiled at her mother's obvious lack of interest in the other candidates. She knew that as far as her mother was concerned there were no other candidates. But privately Karen wasn't as optimistic about her chances. Just because her mother and sister had been queens, there was no guarantee that she'd be elected. People voted for girls for a lot of reasons and family loyalty was only one of them. Charlotte Melville had a lot of relatives in Wilks County and that might help her. For that matter, the fact that the Melville farm was one of the biggest ones in the county wouldn't hurt.

But Karen was determined not to worry about that yet. It was only the first of July and the voting for the contest wouldn't be until August 26. She wasn't going to spend the whole summer worrying. She would do her best and that would have to be good enough.

That was exactly what she told herself the next day when she dressed for the Fourth of July picnic. Each year the town of Wilks had a big picnic in the parking lot of the shopping center on the outskirts of town. The cement parking lot would be covered with people who'd come to enjoy the barbecue dinner sold by the Chamber of Commerce.

At that dinner Karen would make her first official appearance as a contestant for Harvest Queen. She and the other girls would be introduced and each would say a few words. Karen had her short speech memorized and she thought she looked very good in the white cotton piqué dress with the tiny straps that tied on the shoulders. It was an old dress of Lucy's, but that didn't bother Karen. After all, running for Harvest Queen in Wilks County, Kansas, was not the same thing as running for Queen of the Rose Bowl, she thought, though she would not have dared to tell her mother that. Her mother was so excited and happy about the whole thing that Karen was almost glad she'd agreed to run.

The shopping center picnic looked exactly the same to Karen this year as any other year, but her mother insisted there were more people there. Karen saw a lot of people she knew and she spoke politely to all of them. By the time she'd been there an hour, she felt as though her face were frozen into a permanent smile. Nevertheless, she went through the motions with all the grace and courtesy that she'd been taught as a child.

Several people wished her luck and most of them predicted that she would win. It obviously made her mother happy to hear those predictions, but Karen noticed that Charlotte Melville seemed to have as much attention as she did.

At one point, Karen said, "I'm hungry. Let's go eat."

"Not yet," her mother warned. "You might spill barbecue sauce on your dress. You want to look pretty for your speech."

"Mother, it's not a speech," Karen protested. But that was the only protest she made that evening. It was easier to go along and do exactly what people expected of her. So Karen walked around, smiling and chatting with people. Most of the time either Lucy or her mother was with her. She was grateful when Sue showed up. Sue, who was not a member of her family, didn't have to campaign for her. She could be the friend who stuck by her side all the time.

About three thirty, Karen whispered, "Boy, I'm glad you're here. My feet hurt. My face is frozen into a stupid grin and my hand hurts from shaking hands with so many people. Plus I feel like a dope and I'm getting a sunburn. If you weren't here, I'd probably run away."

"You'll speak at four," Sue reminded her quickly.

Karen laughed. "I'm not going to run away, Sue. I promised Mama and Lucy that I'd go through with this. So I will."

"You're doing fine," Sue encouraged her. "Oh, look, there's Pete."

Karen looked over to a group of people on the other side of the parking lot. There was Pete Peterson, looking tall and handsome as he talked with one of the contestants for the contest. Karen's heart did a flip-flop. She said in a small voice, "I thought he was working."

"That's Sarah Weintraub he's talking to," Sue said. "But he's not interested in her. And she won't win the contest."

"You make it sound as if Pete were one of the prizes," Karen said. Then she looked at her friend and realized that somehow Sue *did* believe that. All along, Sue had hinted that Pete would be interested in the girl who won. Was she right? Karen looked across the barbecue tables, past the small groups of people talking to each other, past the picnic benches and table to the place where Pete was standing. Would he be interested in her if she won? It was something to hope for. Something to work for.

As four o'clock approached, Karen began to get nervous. Even though her speech was really only going to be a few words, it would be the first time she'd ever stood in front of this many people and had them look at her. She guessed that there must be close to three hundred people there, and though that wasn't much compared to the town population of thirty-four thousand, it looked like a lot to Karen.

Her mother called her over. Karen stood patiently while her mother applied a bit more blusher and lipstick. She warned Karen to stand tall, smile prettily, and speak loudly.

Karen's knees were shaking as she walked to the small platform where the president of the Chamber of Commerce stood behind a microphone. The steps leading up to the platform felt rickety and Karen wondered for a moment if they might fall. She followed Charlotte Melville up the stairs and Charlotte seemed a little unsteady in her high-heeled sandals. Karen was glad she'd insisted on wearing flats. At least she didn't have to worry about falling. If my knees don't give way, she thought to herself.

The Chamber of Commerce president talked a long time and then he introduced the mayor, who talked even longer. Finally it was time to introduce the candidates for queen. Karen was glad when she realized that he was calling on Wendy Abbot first. Wendy spoke too fast and seemed about ready to run off the stage. She's more scared than I am, Karen thought, and she was ashamed of herself because that made her feel better.

After Wendy came Louisa May Martin. Then it was Charlotte Melville's turn. Next came Sarah Weintraub. Then it was Karen's turn.

Karen held her head high and walked slowly to the microphone. Though she could feel her pulse beating much too quickly, she was careful to keep her voice low and deliberate. Both her mother and Lucy had warned her about speaking too quickly. Karen smiled at the audience before she began. She turned her head slowly from one side to the other, trying to encompass the whole parking lot full of people. Then she said, "Mr. Mayor, President of the Chamber, honored guests: I am very happy to be here today. I'd like to thank my mother, Marsha Williams, and my sister, Lucy Williams, for inviting me." She paused while people laughed. It was no secret in Wilks that her mother and sister were more eager for her to win than anyone. Both of them had been talking about Karen entering the contest for weeks.

A little surprised that she'd been able to ad-lib a joke, Karen went on with her prepared speech. She praised the contest, the parade, the elected officials, the service organizations who sponsored the contestants, and the community as a whole. She ended with, "We live in the prettiest part of the best state in the best nation of the world. If elected, I will be honored to serve as your queen."

Karen had no idea whether the applause she got was more or less than the applause for the other contestants. She was just glad that the ordeal was over. She was also pleased that she hadn't stumbled over the words or forgotten the speech that her mother and sister had worked so hard writing. Best of all, her knees had stopped knocking the minute she'd actually begun talking. Maybe campaigning wasn't going to be as bad as she had thought it would be.

She and the other contestants sat in chairs on the platform until the rest of the ceremony was finished. The Chamber of Commerce president told a few corny jokes and talked about the wonderful future of agriculture and industry in Wilks County. Then, as people began to drift away, the Wilks County High School Band played a selection from Johann Strauss.

Karen tried not to feel impatient, but the music was

really very bad. She entertained herself by looking into the crowd, trying to spot people she knew. Of course, the person who seemed the easiest to see was Pete Peterson. He was standing in the front row, smiling at the candidates. Once Pete raised his hand, pointed in her direction, then pointed at the tables full of barbecue food and shrugged his shoulders in a questioning manner. Karen's heart began to pound faster. Was Pete asking her to eat with him?

By the time the band finished its third number, the only people still standing around the platform were parents of band members or contestants and Pete. Karen wasn't 100 percent positive that Pete was waiting for her, but she hoped so.

Finally the band stopped, trailing off into one long, frail note followed by frailer applause. Karen clapped politely, as did the other queen contestants. Then she quickly stood up. She was the first down the rickety stairs of the platform and Pete was standing there, waiting for her. He said, "Hi, Karen. Want something to eat?"

"I'd love it," Karen answered quickly. "All the time I was on that stage, my stomach was growling so loud I was afraid I'd drown out the band."

Pete laughed and took her hand. "No way. That's one thing you can say for that band. It's loud."

Karen was pleased by Pete's interest in her. Anytime a boy like Pete held hands in public, it was important, Karen told herself. She looked up at him and smiled. "I'm glad you were there. I could see your head above all the others in the crowd." She hoped he wouldn't think it was too forward of her.

He smiled again and squeezed her hand, sending little thrills up her arm. "Wouldn't have missed it," he said. "My girl up there on the stage, looking just as pretty as a picture."

Karen looked up quickly, wondering if he'd really meant that 'My girl' or if it was just a figure of speech. He looked into her eyes and smiled slowly, as he said, "I'm sorry I haven't called you this week. I had to work every night. Miss me?"

Karen blushed. What was she supposed to answer to that question? If she said yes, he'd know how much she'd hoped he would call. If she said no, it would sound as though she didn't want him to call at all. She decided to try and change the subject. She said, "I hope they have some of those hamburgers left. I'm starved."

"More interested in food than love?" Pete teased. "What kind of a girl are you?"

"A hungry one," Karen admitted. And she was pleased to discover that she was completely over her nervousness with Pete. Now that she was talking to him, he seemed less like a romantic hero of her dreams and more like all the other boys in Wilks. He was nice and good-looking, but the fairy tale quality had disappeared completely. Karen wasn't sure whether she was glad or sorry about that.

They walked across the transformed parking lot toward the barbecue table. On the way they passed children riding the small merry-go-round and tiny tots cars that had been brought in especially for tonight. The parking lot was full of people and benches. There were a few booths selling chances to throw baseballs at bowling pins or darts at balloons. Over in one corner, old Mrs. Whitaker was dressed up as a Gypsy and she was reading palms for a dollar.

Since Karen had seen the parking lot dressed up like

this many times before, it held no particular magic. This shopping center was the real center of Wilks these days. The main street of the town was too narrow and run down to attract many customers anymore. It seemed to Karen that ever since she was born she'd been coming to carnivals and barbecue dinners right here. But she knew that wasn't true because the shopping center was only ten years old.

She thought of telling Pete some of what she was thinking and decided against it. Pete wouldn't think her thoughts on the subject of parking lots were very interesting.

When they came to the barbecue table, Karen reached into her purse to find the money to pay for her supper.

Pete said, "I'm buying." He held out a ten-dollar bill.

"I can't let you do that," Karen protested. She didn't add that he hadn't actually asked her for a date. In fact, she was worried that her mother would be angry with her for going off with a boy when she should be paying attention to the people who might vote for her.

"Contestants eat free," the woman taking tickets said briefly.

"Thank you, Mrs. Marshall," Karen said sweetly. She remembered to smile and call the woman by her name. From now on she would have to be especially careful to be polite and attentive to everyone she met. Not that that would be a problem, Karen admitted to herself. Her mother had raised her with a great deal of attention to manners. No matter how tired or pinched for money Marsha Williams was, she'd always had time to teach her girls the very best way she could.

As they moved down the picnic table line, Karen chose food from nearly every offering. By the time they'd reached the end, she was balancing two paper plates piled high with potato salad, olives, baked beans, dill pickles, pickled beets, corn on the cob, jello salad, cranberry mold, fresh peas, green salad. On top of everything lay two hamburgers soaked with barbecue sauce. "We'll come back for dessert," Karen said to the man who piled the last hamburger on her second plate.

"That's what I like to see," Tom Perkins teased. "Pretty girl with a good appetite. Make a good farm wife. You engaged yet?" Tom Perkins was a bachelor of about fifty who lived way out in the country on a huge dairy farm all alone.

Karen smiled at him and answered, "Not yet."

"Wait a minute," Pete broke in with a joking manner. "You stay away from her, Tom. She's my girl." Then he added, "But she's got a sister . . . and a mother."

It was Tom Perkins's turn to look slightly embarrassed and Karen wondered if he could be interested in her mother. After all, he was eligible and her mother was too. Maybe there was a possibility there. Karen would have loved to see her mother happily married. It would be so wonderful for her. Maybe sometime later she would mention Tom to her mother and see what reaction she had. You never knew.

Thinking about her mother made Karen sad and it apparently showed in her face because Pete asked, "What's wrong?"

"Nothing," Karen said quickly. "I guess campaigning is just getting to me a little bit. All these people."

But Pete wasn't really listening to her. He was looking for a place for them to sit and eat. Finally he pointed to an empty spot at the end of one of the long tables. Karen followed him to the bench and sat across from him. She started on the corn on the cob first, then worked her way to the pickled beets. It was a few minutes before she realized that Pete was watching her eat with an amused expression on his face. When she realized he was looking at her, she blushed.

Pete said, "You look cute with a red face and barbecue sauce on your cheek."

She knew she was blushing even more as she looked around for extra napkins. The sauce was sloppy and she thought she must look awful.

Pete handed her a stack of extra napkins from the other side of the table. He said, "Go ahead and eat. You look cute."

She tried to keep on eating, but somehow the food she'd been enjoying so much didn't taste as good to her as it had before. She looked down at the second plate, which was only half gone, and said, "I guess my eyes were bigger than my stomach."

"You did pretty well though," Pete teased. "Want some dessert?"

"Oh, no," Karen said. "I think a walk might be a better idea."

Pete looked at his watch and frowned. He said, "Listen, Karen, I told my Dad I'd go to the station for a couple of hours. Just long enough for him to have some supper. But I'll be back by eight. Okay?"

"Sure," Karen answered. Then she added, "You don't have to come back if you don't want to."

"I'll be back soon," he promised. "We can dance later. There's going to be a disco—right?"

"Right," Karen said. Her head was swimming because of the sudden attention from Pete. He acted as though they had been going together for years. How was she supposed to act?

When Pete left to go to the gas station, Karen looked for her family. Lucy wasn't around and her mother was talking to some people. She saw Sue over on the side of the shopping center talking to some kids. Karen knew she could join that group easily, but she didn't really feel like it. Somehow, now that most of her campaigning was done for the day, the old sadness had returned.

Karen stood back and looked at the scene in front of her. In the dimming afternoon light the parking center looked a lot prettier than it had earlier. There were brightly dressed people and kids running around with balloons. People seemed to be having fun.

Karen saw Sue look over and wave to her, but Sue was far enough away that Karen thought she could pretend she hadn't seen her. Quickly, Karen turned her back and walked away from the picnic tables. She would take a little walk by herself to work off some of that food she'd just eaten. Surely no one would think that was strange.

Karen walked away from the parking lot, down the street, past the smaller shops that lined the highway, and into the unpaved street that led down to the small bridge by the river. She knew her mother would be distressed if she found out that Karen had slipped out of the picnic, but she told herself she would just walk as far as the bridge and turn around and come back. A short walk would be refreshing and she'd be able to face the evening better. As she was making these excuses for herself, Karen wondered again what it was about her that was different from other girls. What girl wouldn't be happy to be campaigning for queen and waiting for Pete to come back to her? What was wrong with her?

The road trailed out into a small path that was seldom used. Since cars couldn't cross the bridge, no one used the road except couples who came down here to make out. Karen had only walked down here once before, when she'd been much younger. But she knew the way, just as she knew nearly every part of Wilks County.

It was quiet now that she was away from the highway. There were no cars to make noise and even the air seemed cleaner. Karen's steps quickened as she neared the river bank. Here it would be cooler and greener. Here she could relax. Maybe she would even take her shoes off and cool her hot feet in the running water. She could hear birds singing and there even seemed to be a breeze.

She wasn't surprised to round the bend and see a car parked at the edge of the road. It had been too much to hope that she'd be totally alone.

She saw Roger long before he saw her. He was down on his hands and knees at the river's edge, pulling something up out of the water. He seemed to have lost something because he was making several attempts to snag whatever it was with a long, crooked stick. Karen watched him quietly, not moving. She didn't want to startle him and ruin his chances of catching whatever it was.

Finally he pulled the stick up out of the water. Karen could see it had a fork on the end of it and at the end of that fork hung a soggy piece of clothing or a cloth. Karen called out, "Hi, Roger. You fishing for old clothes?"

He turned quickly, smiling happily when he saw it was her. "I was curious what it was. I guess it's an old T-shirt. No buried treasure or anything."

Karen walked closer, asking, "Were you fishing?"

"Not really," Roger answered. "I guess I was fishing for ideas. For my poetry," he added.

Karen smiled down at him. Roger was still on his hands and knees. His pant legs were very wet and he looked like a small, naughty boy as he held the stick with the silly prize. She said, "You looked as though you were having fun. I'm sorry I interrupted you."

"Not at all," Roger said. "Want to sit down?"

"Can't," Karen said. "I'm supposed to be back at the picnic. Plus, if I sat down I'd get dirty. Can't get dirty, you know."

"You don't sound as though you're having much fun," Roger said.

"Don't I?" Karen asked. She was surprised that it showed. "I guess I am having fun. At least some fun. It's just that it's hard always being on stage."

"You don't have to be on stage with me," Roger said. "I've already decided to vote for you."

Karen looked at him quickly to see if he were serious or teasing. Somehow she'd never thought of Roger voting at all. It didn't seem as though that would be the sort of thing a kid from Chicago would do. She finally said, "Thank you."

"I know what you mean about being on stage," Roger said. "At least, I know a little bit about it. I sing sometimes and play the guitar. The worst part about it is that feeling that everyone is looking at you, expecting you to be something you aren't. It's like, once you consent to be on stage, you aren't supposed to be real anymore. You're supposed to be a superhuman type who doesn't hurt or anything. Know what I mean?"

Karen looked at Roger with amazement. "Believe me," she said, "I know what you mean. I'm glad I ran into you. At least I know now that I'm not crazy. Someone else has felt the way I feel."

Roger looked pleased at her response but he didn't add anything. She liked that.

Instead he said, "I'll sing you the song about the selkie now if you want. Then you can go back to dry land. Just think of yourself as a sort of magical mermaid creature who lives in the sea. Some of the time you have to go back to land where there are others you love. Either way, it's a sort of in-between existence. But very beautiful, of course."

Karen didn't know what to think about what he was saying. She'd never even thought that boys thought things like that. He was telling her a story that sounded like something you'd read in a book of fairy tales. But the boys she knew didn't sing or read fairy tales or play guitars. She wasn't sure how she felt about that. Before she could think anymore, he began singing to her.

His voice was sweet and low. He began by holding the first few notes very long, pronouncing the words carefully and drawing out the song. Then he repeated it at a faster, sweeter, and higher pace. Karen wondered if that was because there were two ways to sing the song or if that was just what he felt like doing. Then he smiled at her and invited, "Now you sing it with me. You can learn it. It's simple. Come on."

Karen joined in with a small soft voice, following his lead. Together, they sang:

> "I am a woman up on the land.
> I am a Selchie on the sea.
> And when I'm far frae every stand
> My dwelling is in Sule Skerrie."

When they'd finished, Roger looked at her and laughed. He said, "But you sing very well. Do you know a lot of folk songs?"

"No," Karen admitted. "I really don't know many songs except what they taught us in elementary school. No one sings here."

"Ah! But you are wrong," Roger said. "There's a

folk concert next Friday evening at Redding. In fact, I'll be singing there. Want to go?"

Karen blushed at the idea. What would people say if she went to the concert with Roger? Everyone would think she was crazy. She shook her head and said, "I can't. I'll have to help my mother." She hoped and prayed that he wouldn't ask her if she was free on another night. Sometimes boys couldn't take the hint and asked her out several times. She hated that, but at sixteen, she'd already learned that it was better to discourage them in the beginning than to go out with them and then have to discourage them later. Besides, when she dated a boy who wasn't popular, Sue and her other friends always made fun of her. They called her Softhearted Karen or other names like that. She hated that more than saying no to the boys.

But Roger didn't ask her to go out any other night. If he was hurt by her refusal, he didn't show it. Instead he said, "Sometime I'll teach you some other songs. You have a nice voice."

Karen answered, "That would be fun. Now I've got to get back to the picnic. It was good to talk with you."

"Yes," Roger said. "I enjoyed it too. See you soon." Then he grinned and added, "In fact, I might show up at the picnic a little later."

"Good," Karen said. "I have a date with Pete and there are a lot of kids you know there." She hoped he would understand what she was saying to him, which was that she liked him but she wasn't interested in dating him. Karen knew she was better at handling situations like this than most girls because her mother had been so careful about teaching her manners. Also, Lucy coached her a lot.

Karen smiled at Roger and turned around. She was aware that his eyes followed her as she walked down the dirt road toward the highway. She was glad that she was wearing a white dress that showed off her tan and that the full skirt made her waist look tiny. She had to laugh at herself because she knew that Roger was the one person who probably didn't notice things like that.

When she got back to the picnic everyone was looking for her. Sue and her mother scolded her but Pete and Lucy just looked worried. Karen only told them, "I felt like taking a walk. There are too many people here."

She was hoping they wouldn't ask her any more than that. She was also hoping that her mother would get over being angry quickly. She hated to hurt her mother or make her angry.

They had started playing the music through the loudspeaker. Pete asked her to dance and she followed him to the center of the roped-off area that had been designated the dance floor. After Pete, several other men asked her to dance because it was the custom to dance with the contestants on that evening. By the time the first intermission arrived Karen had danced every dance, and she was having the best time she'd had all day. She loved to dance so it was no chore—even with the worst dancers among those who asked her.

Karen noticed that both Lucy and her mother danced a lot that evening also. It did Karen good to see that her mother was laughing so much. She also noticed that her mother danced three times with Tom Perkins. Could there be a romance blooming there?

Karen danced with Pete more than anyone else. Roger arrived at the dance about an hour after it started. Karen danced with him once and then he returned to the group of friends with her. She said, "Roger, you remember Sue and Louise and Pete and Sam."

"Of course," Roger said. Then he turned to Sue and asked, "Would you like to dance?"

Sue answered, "No thanks. That's not the right music."

Roger didn't ask Louise or Karen to dance but stayed and talked a few minutes with the group. Then he smiled and said to Karen, "I guess I'll go along now. Thanks for the dance."

They watched Roger leave the group and before he was very far away, Sue said, "I wasn't going to dance with that creep."

"He's not a creep," Karen said hotly. "He's one of the nicest people I've ever met."

Pete and Sue and the others laughed nervously and changed the subject. Karen could tell they thought she was crazy for defending Roger, but she didn't care. He was nice. In fact, there were times when she liked him a whole lot better than Sue. But not as much as Pete, she reminded herself. There was absolutely no one in the world she liked as much as Pete. He was the most special, the very best of all.

5

Karen saw a lot of Pete the next week. He came over to the house every night and sometimes he called her once or twice during the day. All those years that she'd worshiped him from afar, she'd thought of him as some sort of very special and remote hero. Now that she was getting to know him, she liked him even better.

One night they drove out to the lake. On another night Pete took her to the movies. Most of the time they just sat on the couch in Karen's apartment, watching television and talking to Karen's sister and mother. She was glad that her mother and Lucy both thought that Pete was a nice boy.

Though Karen was delighted that Pete was paying so much attention to her, Sue seemed even more delighted. Every morning she called to demand a detailed account of Karen's date with Pete the night before. "Did he kiss you?" Sue would ask.

"Yes," Karen answered.

"Did you like it?"

"Of course," Karen replied. She usually tried to change the subject as quickly as possible because she didn't like talking about such personal things to Sue. Besides, though she liked kissing Pete, she wasn't sure that her reaction was as strong as Sue seemed to expect.

The next time that Sue began to question her about her dates with Pete, Karen turned the tables. She asked, "How about you, Sue? You never talk about your romance. Do you like kissing John?"

"Of course," Sue answered quickly. But the way Sue answered made Karen wonder if she were telling the truth. Sue never really talked much about John, though they'd been going steady for two years. They usually dated once or twice a week, and the rest of the time John worked on his cars. He and his uncle collected old cars and rebuilt them. Karen thought John was kind of dull, but naturally she had never said that to Sue.

"We should try to double-date," Karen said. She thought it would be nice to have another couple along sometimes when she was with Pete.

"Sure," Sue said. "Let's do that."

The opportunity arose much sooner than either girl expected. That evening Pete told Karen, "A customer gave me four tickets to a concert tomorrow night. It's in Redding. Do you want to go?"

"Roger Micklovich is singing," Karen told Pete. And then she blushed. Would Pete wonder how she knew that? She would hate Pete to be jealous of her.

"Is he?" Pete asked. "Then it might be fun to hear someone we know. I don't know much about folk music, but the tickets are free."

63

"The gas isn't," Karen reminded him. "Redding is at the other end of the county."

"That's okay," Pete said. "Want to ask Sue and John?"

Karen went right to the telephone and called Sue, who called John and then called Karen back. Within an hour they'd made a plan that included a picnic at the concert.

The next evening was a warm July night. Karen wore the white piqué dress she'd worn at the picnic. She pulled her auburn hair back and tied a pink ribbon around it. At the waist of the dress she pinned real pink roses and she was wearing rose perfume that Lucy had given her. She felt very beautiful and very grown up. After all, she was going out with Pete Peterson, the boy she'd been in love with for years. It was a special occasion.

The drive to Redding was long and dull. The flat Kansas fields were bright green, but the corn was so high you couldn't see above the stalks. Karen felt as though they'd been driving forever and not getting anywhere. All the fields looked exactly alike. Pete and John talked a lot about cars and Sue pretended to be interested. Karen didn't know enough about cars to even pretend. She couldn't even drive yet. Lucy and her mother shared one broken-down old Oldsmobile and Karen hadn't bothered to learn to drive. One of these days, she told herself.

By the time they got to Redding her roses were wilted and her hair had blown out of the pink ribbon. The white piqué dress felt damp and wilted too. After all, she thought fretfully, it's only a hand-me-down. And Pete hadn't told her she looked pretty. Maybe she didn't.

They were late, so their picnic was hurried. Karen

ate one egg salad sandwich and drank a glass of lemonade. She passed up the cake and fruit because there really wasn't time. They had to hurry to get to their seats before the concert began.

The concert took place in a high school football stadium. They found seats halfway up the bleachers. By the time they sat down, the first singer had begun. It was a girl with long, straight blond hair who had a high, sweet voice. Karen loved listening to her, but John obviously didn't. He was sitting beside Karen and twitched and turned all during the performance.

The next singer was a black woman who sang some old blues songs. Karen had never heard anything like it. The woman's voice was strong and powerful. When she sang, she sang very loudly, and the music seemed to float up to the very top of the bleachers. Her first song was long and sad and Karen felt tears come to her eyes. She turned to Pete, who was on her left, and asked, "Isn't she wonderful?"

Pete looked surprised and said, "I guess so. She sounds kind of funny to me."

Karen was disappointed that he didn't like the music better. She thought it was wonderful. But at least Pete didn't complain as John did. During the intermission, John tried to get them to go home. "But I want to hear Roger sing," Karen objected. "Aren't you interested in hearing him?"

"Sure," Pete agreed quickly, and Karen flashed him a warm thank-you smile.

Roger was the first performer in the second part of the performance. He looked very cool and self-assured as he came out to the center of the platform they'd erected as a temporary stage. Karen couldn't help remembering how she'd felt last week on a stage that looked a lot like this one. Was Roger feeling the same butterflies in his stomach? If so, he certainly didn't show it.

He was wearing a white dress shirt that was open at the neck. The cuffs were open and rolled up. He looked very nice, Karen decided, and she leaned forward eagerly to hear what he would sing.

His first song was a love ballad about a young woman whose lover was untrue. It was very sad and sweet. Karen thought it was beautiful, but several people around her seemed to grow restless as the verses went on and on. She was glad when he followed that song with a small joke and then said, "Now the next one is faster, so those of you who are asleep, time to wake up." That song was a sea chantey, and by the time he finished singing it people in the audience were clapping their hands.

Next he led everyone in several verses of "Old MacDonald Had a Farm," and he made all the funny noises for the animals himself. Karen was laughing so hard at the sight of Pete trying to imitate Roger's oink-oinks and hee-haws that she had to wipe tears from her eyes. He left the platform then to the accompaniment of loud applause. Pete and John were among those who clapped loudly and called for an encore.

Roger did come back briefly, bowing to the waist and settling down comfortably on his high stool. Then he looked up at the audience and said, "I'd like to dedicate this next number to a young woman who will be the next Queen of the Harvest in Wilks County—Karen Williams. And I'd like to have Karen stand up and take a bow."

Karen was amazed that Roger would ask her to stand in front of such a large crowd. The blood ran to her face and her first impulse was to run away. But Pete and Sue both whispered to her to stand up quickly. She stood and waved her arm broadly, as Lucy and her mother had showed her. As she waved, she told herself that Roger was trying to be helpful. Still, she would have liked one day without having to think about campaigning.

Roger smiled up at her and said, "There she is, folks, my candidate for queen—Karen Williams. I hope she'll be yours." Then he sang the soft and haunting song he'd sung to her at the bridge a week ago. Karen felt her flushed face go pale and her knees grow weak as he sang the song. How did he dare to sing that song to all these people? It had seemed so private and special when he'd sung it to her alone, but now it just seemed cheap.

When the song was over, Karen sat down. Sue looked at her, leaning across John to say over the clapping, "Wow! That will really help your campaign. I guess being nice to him was a good idea."

Karen nodded weakly. Her feelings were so mixed up that she wasn't even sure what she did feel anymore. In fact, she was beginning to wonder if any of her feelings were to be trusted. She decided not to worry about it and just try to enjoy the rest of the program. But she couldn't help letting her thoughts drift back to Roger and his performance. Why had he done such a public thing? It must not have meant much to him when he'd sung that song just to her. Then she chided herself for being critical of Roger. In truth, it wasn't until he'd begun to sing in public that she'd realized how much that moment by the bridge had meant to her. As usual, she was all mixed up.

After the concert, they went down to the platform to see Roger. Karen noticed that Sue was a lot more friendly to Roger than she had been before. Roger thanked them for coming, adding, "I hope that my little plug helped you, Karen. I'd like to see you win, if that's what you want?" There was a slight lilt at the end of his sentence and Karen wondered if she was expected to answer the question.

Did she want to win? That was another thing she just wasn't sure about. But at least she didn't have to answer him because Sue was so busy talking that no one else had a chance. Sue thought that Roger might be able to help Karen with her campaign. She asked him, "Would you be willing to make a few public appearances with Karen? Sing some of your funnier songs?"

"Oh, Sue," Karen objected. "Roger is a professional performer. You can't ask him to do that."

"She just *did* ask me," Roger pointed out reasonably. Then he added, "I'd like to say yes, if it's all right with you, Karen. I'd like to help."

"Of course it's all right," Karen answered. "You're really wonderful."

"Good," Pete said. He reached over and shook Roger's hand in a firm and grown-up manner. "Then you'll come to Karen's birthday party next Friday night? We blast off the campaign then. I'm general chairman."

Sue and Karen looked at Pete, trying to keep the surprise and amusement out of their faces. It was the first that anyone had heard about Pete being general chairman. But, of course, no one was going to contradict him. In fact, Karen was very pleased that Pete showed so much interest in her campaign. The fact that it might have been motivated by a touch of jealousy didn't seem to bother her at all.

6

For the first time in her life Karen dreaded her birthday party. She would be seventeen and she knew she should be feeling very grown up and together. Instead she felt younger and more insecure than she could ever remember. Her feelings had been so mixed up all week that she wondered what could be wrong with her.

Part of the time she dreaded the possibility that she might win the Harvest Queen contest and part of the time she dreaded the possibility of losing. Part of the time she thought Sue was a wonderful friend and part of the time she was angry at her for being so bossy. It was the same with her feelings about her mother and sister, though Karen never doubted that she loved them. The worst part of that whole week was the doubts she had about her romance with Pete.

If Pete was the man of her dreams, then why did she think so much about Roger? What was it about that tall, slim stranger that made her think about him? How could she be dating Pete and dreaming of Roger? And why? Everyone agreed that Pete was the best catch in town, while Roger—at least, according to Wilks County standards—was no catch at all.

As she put on her makeup, getting ready for the party, she realized that she looked sad. What good is it to dress up if you don't smile? Karen asked herself. As she painted her mouth with a pale coral lipstick, she smiled at herself in the mirror. She reminded herself that everyone had worked very hard to make this party a success. It wouldn't be if she were morose or difficult.

Since the party was at Sue's house, Karen felt almost as though it were for someone else, especially since some of the people who attended weren't even friends of hers. Sue had invited some of her father's influential friends and even a newspaper reporter, in the hope that it would help Karen's campaign.

There was punch and cake laid out on a long table that was covered by a white lace tablecloth. Sue insisted that Karen stand at one end of the table and shake hands with people before they came to pick up their refreshments. Karen was overwhelmed and dismayed by the formality of the setup. She whispered to Sue in an angry voice, "You promised it would just be a few people."

"Stand up straight and smile," Sue whispered back.

Karen felt a flash of anger at her friend's bossiness. Why did Sue insist on treating her as though she were a paper doll to be pushed around to suit her plans? Usually Karen let her friend make the plans, but now she felt too uncomfortable. "I'm not going to stand there like a dummy," Karen said. "It looks too silly."

Sue glared at her but said nothing else as Karen moved away from the table and began to circulate with her guests. She moved from one group to another, trying to be friendly. She saw that her mother and Lucy were trying hard also. But instead of enjoying the excitement, they just looked tired and anxious. Why am I doing this? Karen asked herself for the hundredth time.

The party dragged on but never really got started. In a way, Karen was glad that it was such an obvious flop but she hated to let Sue down. When more than half the people had shaken her hand and gone away, Karen began to relax a little bit. Now that most of the folks she didn't know were gone, it felt more like a real birthday party. She saw Roger talking to John over in one corner of the room. She made her way across Sue's large living room to talk with them.

Roger was alone by the time she reached him. He seemed glad to see her. He took her hand for a moment, smiled at her, and asked, "Do you know you look like a princess in a fairy tale today?"

Karen looked down at the simple blue dress she was wearing. It was really very plain with small cap sleeves and a deep-cut heart-line neck. She'd chosen it at least partly because it had been inexpensive. Karen winced as she thought of the amount of money her mother and sister were spending on this campaign. Yet they were spending much less than most of the contestants, partly because they didn't have it and partly because Karen kept insisting that a simple campaign would work just as well.

In response to Roger's compliment, she said, "Thank you."

"I don't suppose you're interested in kissing any frogs?" Roger asked softly. The look in his eyes told her that his question was serious.

She decided to handle it as though it were a joke. "I hear it's a girl's job to kiss lots of frogs before she finds a prince. Isn't that what they say?"

Roger grinned and squeezed her hand tighter. Karen was surprised at the sudden and quick response she felt to his touch. Why was it that a simple touch of the hand from Roger could make her feel like this? It was Pete she was in love with, wasn't it?

Before she had time to worry much about her surprising reaction, Sue called across the room to her. Her friend's voice was sharp and Karen knew she would have to obey or Sue would be angry again. She smiled apologetically at Roger and said, "Duty calls."

"Oh? I thought her name was Sue."

Karen laughed, caught by a mixture of confusing emotions. She laughed so loudly that tears came to her eyes and she had to double up to keep her stomach from hurting. Roger shook his head and said, "It wasn't that funny."

"Yes it was," Karen said, wiping the tears from her eyes. "Besides, I've been so uptight all day, I needed a good laugh."

"That's what frog princes are good for," Roger assured her solemnly. "I hear that beautiful princesses like to keep them around for laughs."

He was still holding her hand and Karen was beginning to feel uncomfortable. Sue was glaring at her from across the room and she wanted to have Roger let go of her hand without having to pull it away.

Roger dropped her hand and asked softly, "Want to go for a drive with me tomorrow night?"

"Yes," Karen whispered back. She felt as though she

were doing something almost sneaky to be making a date with Roger. What would Sue say if she knew? What if Pete found out? "That would be nice," she said. "Pick me up at eight?"

Roger nodded quickly and she walked away from him before she could think about what she'd done. It was crazy, wasn't it? Making a date with Roger when she was in love with Pete?

7

Even though they were just going for a ride, Karen dressed carefully for her date with Roger. She chose her white slacks and yellow cotton sweater. At the last minute she borrowed Lucy's yellow sandals with the high heels.

"You and Pete going someplace special?" Lucy asked.

"Pete has to work this evening," Karen answered. She tried to keep her voice regular as she added, "I'm just going for a ride with Roger."

"Roger? Is he that nice one with the guitar?" Lucy asked. "The one from Chicago?"

Karen nodded and pretended to yawn. "He's asked me to show him around. I said I would."

"Just a platonic relationship, huh?" When Karen nodded her head in agreement, Lucy teased, "Then why the high-heeled shoes? And isn't that my best perfume I smell?"

The doorbell rang before Karen could think of an answer, so she escaped her sister's sharp questions gratefully.

She wasn't the only one who was dressed up. Karen noticed that Roger was wearing his usual white shirt with the rolled-up sleeves, but he had changed from Levis to a pair of dress pants. That made Karen feel a little uncomfortable. None of the boys around this part of Kansas ever wore anything but Levis. Karen found herself hoping that no one would see her out with Roger. He was just too different and she was almost sorry she'd said she'd go for a ride with him.

He was driving a perfectly normal Ford sedan. She thought of Pete's darling little yellow and black Volkswagen Beetle as she climbed into Roger's brown car. At least in this way Roger was a conformist. He held the car door for her though, and that was certainly unusual. Karen wished that he weren't so polite. It would make her less uncomfortable.

"Want to go to the lake?" Roger asked. "We could get a hamburger at Jack's At The Beach."

"Oh, no," Karen said quickly. She certainly didn't want to go to Jack's, where they would surely run into people they knew. "It's such a nice night," she said. "Let's go someplace different."

"Okay," Roger said easily. "But I'll have to get some gas. I'm sorry, but I was afraid I'd be late. Hope you don't mind."

Karen felt her heart begin racing and her face flush with confusion. Was Roger going to go to Pete's gas station? Would he do that? She would absolutely hate him forever if he did that to her. She was about ready to

75

tell him that she'd rather go to Jack's when she realized that he was taking a different street. With relief, Karen saw that Roger was swinging into a different gas station. What had ever made her think he would be so insensitive as to go to Pete's station? Roger was too nice a person for that.

After the tank was filled, Roger asked, "Where to? Your wish is my command."

"How about Wilsonville?" Karen asked. "It's a pretty drive and there's a cute little place down by the river. Want to go there?"

"Wilsonville, it is," Roger said. "Of course, I have no idea *where* it is. You'll have to give me directions."

Thirty minutes later they were sitting inside a little cafe in Wilsonville. The table had a red-and-white-checked cloth on it and there was an old wine bottle that held a candle. Roger looked around and said, "This reminds me of a place I used to go to in Chicago."

"Why did you leave Chicago?" Karen asked. She hoped the question wasn't too nosy, but she wondered. Roger had moved to Wilks about four months ago with his mother and father. From what she'd heard, Roger's mother was a well-known designer and his father was retired.

"My folks had a dream," Roger explained briefly. "Ever since I was a kid they've talked of moving to the country. My dad's writing a book and my mother is learning to bake bread."

"I've seen your mother around town. She looks so sophisticated."

Roger laughed at the idea. "Sophisticated? Not really. In fact, you remind me a little of my mother. At least, when you laugh. You both have very deep, full laughs. Wonderful sound."

Karen flushed with distress. After the birthday party yesterday, both her mother and Sue had told her not to laugh in public anymore. Sue said she sounded crude and her mother said it sounded a bit loud. Now here was Roger saying it was a wonderful sound. She wished she could believe him.

Their drinks came and they talked of other things. Karen told Roger about herself, about her life and her family. Roger told her about his school in Chicago, about his music, and about his older brother who was in medical school. By the time they left the restaurant, Karen felt as though she'd known Roger for a long, long time.

He opened the car door for her again, taking her hand briefly to help her inside. Again Karen felt a slight shiver as she responded to the warmth of his touch. She found herself wondering what it would be like to kiss Roger. Would it feel good to be held in his arms?

"Cold?" he asked.

"Not really," Karen answered. "I guess it was just a reaction to coming outdoors."

On the way home from Wilsonville, Roger asked, "How about the future, Karen? What's the future hold for you?"

Karen looked out the window, staring at the corn-fields that seemed to whiz past her window. "I'm not sure," she said. "Right now I'm just concentrating on getting through the summer."

"But beyond that?" Roger asked. Karen thought his voice sounded slightly impatient with her. "Where will you go to college?"

"I'm not sure I will," Karen confessed. She struggled

for words to explain. "Mostly kids around here don't go to college. My sister wanted to, but it didn't work out."

"Lucy wanted to go to college?" Roger asked. His voice sounded surprised.

"She was a better student than I am," Karen said. Her voice was trailing off and she was still looking out into the black farmland as though she were talking to herself or to the wind. "Yes, Lucy was a really good student. We thought she'd get a scholarship to the university. And she did, but she didn't go."

"What happened?" Roger asked.

"I don't know exactly," Karen confessed. "It just didn't seem to work out. My mom had to work nights and I would have been home alone. Oh, they probably could have worked that out, but they didn't. Anyway, Lucy got that job in the bank and she's been there ever since." Suddenly Karen felt a wave of sadness wash over her. She finished, "I guess Lucy just thought it was easier to stay home than to go. Sometimes it's easier not to try."

"Never!" Roger disagreed sharply. His voice was harsh and clear as he said, "No one should ever give up without trying. Never!"

Karen looked over at her date. Why was he so excited about that statement? What had happened to him to make him so sure it was better to fight? She wanted to ask him why he was so definite, but the tone of his voice warned her away.

She waited for him to say something else, but he didn't. They drove in silence for a few minutes and then he said, "I think I'll teach you a song. Do you know you have a very nice voice?"

They spent the next half hour laughing and singing,

and before she knew it they were sitting in front of Karen's house. She turned to Roger and held out her hand. "I had a wonderful time," she said.

Roger nodded and asked, "Want to do this again sometime? With practice you could learn to carry a tune."

"Yes," Karen said. Then she added, "Sometime." Though she had enjoyed her date with Roger, she knew in her heart that it was Pete she really cared about. Roger was a nice person and she enjoyed talking to him, but it was Pete she'd been attracted to since the first grade.

Under the light of the streetlight, Roger's face seemed to register disappointment for a second. Then he squeezed her hand and said, "Good. I'll look forward to that."

Before she realized that he wasn't even going to try and kiss her, Roger had opened the car door for her. He walked her to the door, smiled quickly, and turned away. Karen stood on the step of her apartment building, holding her key in her hand. She was surprised that Roger had left her so quickly and just a bit put out that he hadn't at least tried to kiss her. Not that she would have let him, Karen told herself. After all, she was Pete's girl.

That night she had a hard time going to sleep. She kept going over and over the conversation she'd had with Roger. She kept coming back to his sharp reaction to the idea of taking the easy way out. What was behind his sudden change of mood?

Though she found Roger intriguing, there was no comparison between Roger and Pete, Karen told herself. Pete was much better looking. He was just as nice and a whole lot more her type. A boy like Roger would never understand a small-town girl like her. Roger would be going back to Chicago after he graduated from high school in June. Karen was sure he would go to college. And she—she would be right here in Wilks. With Pete, she reminded herself, and curled up against her bed pillow to sleep.

8

It seemed to Karen that Lucy called her just a few minutes after she'd fallen asleep. At the sound of her sister's voice, Karen groaned, opened one eye, saw that it was eight o'clock, and rolled over. It took Lucy several more minutes to convince her that she should get up.

Pulling on her terry cloth robe, Karen walked into the kitchen, growling, "What's the big hurry? This is summer vacation." Immediately she felt guilty because Lucy didn't have a vacation at all this year. She'd had to take her two weeks last spring when her mother was sick.

But Lucy didn't take offense. She just smiled cheerfully and said, "Don't blame me. It's your best buddy on the telephone. She says it's important."

"Sue?" Karen asked. Before Lucy could answer, she

put the telephone to her ear and said, "Hi, Sue. What's up?"

"I saw you," Sue said dramatically. "And I must say it was the dumbest thing I can imagine. What if Pete finds out?"

"Sue, did you wake me up to bawl me out?" Karen asked. "Because if you did, I'm going back to bed."

"Karen! This is serious. Promise me you won't go out with Roger again and I promise you I won't tell Pete."

Karen couldn't keep the anger out of her voice. "That sounds like blackmail to me," she said. "I don't feel like being blackmailed so early in the morning. Tell Pete if you want to. And I'll go out with Roger whenever I feel like it." She hung up the telephone before Sue could say anything else.

Karen poured herself a cup of coffee and sat down across from Lucy. Lucy asked, "You got troubles with the troops, General?"

"Sort of," Karen admitted. "Sue thinks I've made a big mistake dating Roger. I suppose Pete would be mad if he knew, but I'm not sure I care."

"You kind of like Roger, don't you?" Lucy asked.

Karen frowned and shook her head. "I know it's Pete for me, but it is fun to talk with a boy who's been somewhere and done something different. I love Wilks and all the people here, but sometimes I wish I knew more about the rest of the world. Do you ever feel that way?"

Lucy made a face and said, "Honey, I feel that way nearly every day of my life."

Karen thought of her conversation with Roger last night. Somehow she'd always thought of Lucy as being beautiful and popular. It was a new idea to think of Lucy as someone who might have other dreams—

dreams that had failed. She asked, "Lucy, why didn't you go to college?"

Lucy smiled quickly, stood up, rinsed out her cup, and said, "Got to get to the salt mine, sweetie. See you tonight. Don't let Sue get you down. You have a right to your own life, you know."

"So why didn't you go to college?" Karen persisted.

Lucy's smile faded. "It was complicated. Some of it seemed so important then and it turned out it really wasn't at all. There was a boy I was dating who didn't want me to go. You were very young and needed someone to look after you. Mama would have missed me—oh, Karen, I'm really not sure. All I know is I didn't go and I've been sorry ever since."

Karen was surprised at the look of pain on her sister's face. She had no idea that Lucy felt so strongly about the missed opportunity. She said, "You could go now. Take the money Aunt Alice left us and go to the city. Go to school at night if you have to, but go to school."

Lucy shook her head, put her cup in the cupboard, and kissed her sister on the cheek. "Lost time never returns. I'm too old to go to college now. By the time I got out I'd be thirty."

Karen stared at her empty coffee cup and thought about the things that Lucy had said. It was disturbing to think of Lucy as someone who had been disappointed by life. Then her thoughts strayed to her mother. Her mother's marriage had been a failure. Karen couldn't remember her father very well, but everything she'd heard convinced her that they were better off without him. Would her own life be disappointing?

Quickly, Karen shook her head and stood up. She wasn't going to ruin her day worrying about things she couldn't control. She was going to do something that was fun and forget about all the world's troubles. Then she groaned. Today was the day she'd promised Sue and her mother that she would begin going door to door.

Can't do that, Karen told herself. Sue won't be over being mad at me for at least a week. Long experience had taught her that. She almost smiled as she realized that her argument with Sue had postponed her door-to-door campaign indefinitely. Of all the things they'd planned for her to do, that was the one she hated the most. Somehow the idea of knocking on people's doors and asking them to vote for her was too terrible. Well, it couldn't be helped. She would just have to spend the day reading or cleaning house.

But Karen was wrong about Sue being mad for a week. Only three days later she called and started talking about the campaign as though nothing had happened. Karen didn't bring up the subject of Roger and neither did Sue. Instead they talked about her first appearance at the shopping mall the next week.

"You'll have a lot of practice before then," Sue said. "You're going to social functions nearly every night for the next two weeks."

"I know," Karen said. She didn't bother to complain. No one seemed to think it was anything but odd that she wasn't overjoyed by her constant round of socializing. It never seemed to occur to her mother or Sue or Pete that she might not like meeting people and talking about things she had no interest in. Besides, she was sure she was getting fat from eating all the party food at the meetings and suppers she was attending.

Even though she was determined not to complain, Karen couldn't avoid arguing with Sue. This time her mother and sister were in on it, too. They were all driving to a Wilks County 4–H bean supper over in another small town about thirty minutes away. Sue was talking about the campaign and she said, "I figure tomorrow would be a good day to start going door to door. How about if we start in your own neighborhood?"

"I'm not going to do door-to-door campaigning," Karen said.

"You have to!" Sue said indignantly.

"Are you sure?" Lucy asked her sister.

"I really think you should," her mother urged.

Karen took a deep breath and explained as gently as she could, "I know you think it's important, but I just can't do it. I tried on my own last week—just to see how I would feel. I went to Mrs. Persip's house and knocked on the door. Now I've known Mrs. Persip all my life, but when she opened that door I wanted to run away. Instead of asking her to vote for me, I asked her if she wanted anything from the store."

"That's good," Sue said. "It will get you votes."

Karen shook her head. "Try and listen, Sue. The point is, I couldn't ask Mrs. Persip to vote for me. Remember when we were little? We would go out to sell Girl Scout cookies and I could never talk? You had to sell all the cookies. Well, it was the same that day. I just can't do it."

"You're not a Girl Scout now," Sue said shortly.

"I'm sorry," Karen said. "I hate to disappoint you all. I know you want me to win. And I think I will win anyway—at least, I hope I will win. But win or lose, I can't go door to door. I just can't."

They were at the 4–H supper parking lot by now and Karen was afraid she was going to burst into tears. Her mother must have sensed her mood because she leaned over from the front seat and patted Karen on the shoulder. Her mother said, "You'll win. Don't worry about that. And if you don't want to do door-to-door campaigning yet, you don't have to. No one is going to make you."

Blinking back the tears, Karen smiled gratefully at her mother. She determined that she would do her very best to make it up to her by campaigning extra hard tonight and every other night that she had to attend one of these gatherings.

Actually, Karen didn't mind the suppers. It was fun to be the center of attention and talk to people she'd known since she was a little girl. She always got a kick out of having Lucy and her mother by her side. Invariably, people would talk about what beautiful queens they had been.

Tonight Tom Perkins was one of the guests and Karen noticed that her mother and Tom spent a lot of time talking to each other. Karen whispered to Lucy, "Do you think Mama might be interested in him?"

Lucy looked over at her mother speculatively and then shrugged. "Maybe. But I'm not sure Mama would ever take another chance."

The Williams women aren't chance takers, Karen thought. Before she could pursue the thought, a woman who worked in the bank with Lucy came over to talk to her. After that, Karen was so busy campaigning that she didn't think any more about her mother or Tom Perkins.

After the supper, at nine thirty, Pete came in the door. Karen looked up and smiled gratefully at him. One of the reasons that campaigning had been as easy as it was was because of Pete. Nearly every night he found a way to get to wherever she was. Usually she rode home with him.

This evening he got there in time to have coffee and cake. Within minutes, Sue had made him promise to take the day off to come to the shopping center with them. "Lucy and Mrs. Williams both have to work," Sue said. "I'm afraid that Karen will back out unless you and I are there."

Karen was so glad to see Pete that she didn't mind Sue's comments as much as she might have. She smiled at her friend and objected mildly, "You make me sound as though I were a juvenile delinquent or something."

Sue didn't say anything and Karen realized that in Sue's eyes she was. They'd never talked again about her date with Roger and Karen was happy enough about that. At least part of her reluctance to talk about the date was because Roger had never called her again. Funny how mistaken she'd been about that. Usually a girl could tell, and Karen had honestly thought that Roger was interested in her. But it had been a week and a half now, and obviously he wasn't. If he had been interested, he would have called, wouldn't he?

"We don't really need Roger," Sue said. Karen was startled. Had Sue read her thoughts?

"No," Pete agreed quickly. "A lot of people might think his music is weird."

"I'm going to ask him," Karen said quickly. She said it in a voice that she knew sounded firm.

Neither Sue nor Pete argued with her. As they were walking out the door that evening, Karen realized that she'd won two arguments in one day. That was a new experience and she liked it. She wasn't going to go door to door and she was going to invite Roger to play at her campaign day in the shopping center. Now her only problem was whether or not Roger would come. Why hadn't he called her?

As she was riding home with Pete, she was thinking of Roger. Quickly, she shook her head and turned her attention to Pete, asking, "Work hard today?"

"Gas station was busy," Pete answered. He dropped his arm across her shoulder and asked comfortably, "How about you? Work hard?"

"Not exactly," Karen said. "But I had a good day." She was thinking of the way she seemed to be learning to stand up for herself. Roger would approve of that. Did Pete? She glanced sideways at the tall blond boy beside her. Here she was sitting beside the boy she'd dreamed about all these years and she was thinking of someone else. What was wrong with her?

"I love you," Pete said lightly.

Karen felt her heart begin to beat louder. The blood seemed to race through her veins. Had she heard correctly? Was Pete really saying what she thought she heard?

He pulled her closer to him as he turned the corner and headed toward her house. Once parked, he turned toward her, kissed her gently, and whispered, "I've wanted to tell you from the first. I love you, Karen, and I want you to be my girl."

Karen opened her mouth, not sure of exactly what she would say. Any girl in her right mind would be thrilled to have Pete Peterson say those words to her. But somehow she wasn't. What was wrong with her anyway?

She looked up at the moon overhead. "It's a sliver now. Soon it will be full. A harvest moon. Remember that song?"

"No," Pete admitted. "I guess you think I'm a clod not to know more about poetry or songs than I do. I guess you think I just fell off the turnip truck or something."

Karen laughed. "I don't think you're a clod, Pete. I think you're a very nice boy."

He held her tighter, pulling her toward him in a

demanding way, and said in a deep voice, "Man, not boy. I'm eighteen years old."

Karen laughed, pulling away from him and quickly opening the car door. "You'll always be a boy to me, Pete. I remember you in kindergarten. You had a fight with Riley Wilson. First day."

"And you wore a bright pink dress with ribbons on it," Pete countered. "You were the prettiest girl in class. Still are."

Karen leaned over, kissed him softly. "If I want to stay the prettiest, I've got to get some beautiful sleep. Beautiful sleep for beauty—that's what Mama told me in those days." She slipped out of the car before Pete could reach for her again.

But no matter what she tried that night, she couldn't get to sleep. Her mind went round and round, going over the day's events. She thought about Lucy and college, about her mother and Tom Perkins, about the 4–H supper, and about Sue. Most of all, she thought about Pete's declaration that he loved her. Well aware that she hadn't told him the same thing, Karen asked herself over and over if she did love him. Of course I do, she reminded herself. I've always loved Pete. Haven't I?

9

The day Karen was scheduled to campaign in the shopping center began well enough, but Karen couldn't get over the feeling that it was really going to be awful. "What are you worried about?" Sue asked. "The sky is sunny. Our booth looks great. Relax. Everything is going to be all right."

Karen had to admit that the table and booth that Pete had constructed the night before did look good. And Sue had been right when she insisted that it was better to cover the table with a flowered sheet than to try and use crepe paper. Besides, Karen hoped the sheet would be a salvageable expense, while the paper would have cost just as much and been only good for one day.

Karen smoothed down the pleats of her new yellow dress and wet her lips in an attempt to keep her smile

looking bright and cheerful. No matter how well prepared she was, no matter how much help Sue and Pete
had been, she couldn't get over worrying about the
ordeal that was coming up. Standing in a shopping
center from nine in the morning until nine at night was
certainly not Karen's idea of fun.

Sue smiled as she ran her fingers through the card-
board box of buttons that said "Queen Karen" on
them. Once again, Karen asked, "Are you sure you
didn't pressure your dad to pay for those?"

Sue raised her hand and arm up in the Girl Scout
pledge gesture. "I swear, it was all his idea. No one else
even thought of buttons. Put yours on."

"I shouldn't have to wear one," Karen said quickly.
"I'm the candidate." When she saw the disappointed
look on Sue's face, she immediately capitulated.
"Maybe I should," she said. "Do you think blue or
green would look best?"

"Green," Sue said quickly, obviously pleased for
once to win the argument.

Karen pinned the green button on her shoulder and
tried hard to look cheerful as the first people who
worked in the stores in the shopping mall came across
the parking lot, passing by the booth. Most of them
walked very quickly, not looking at Karen's booth or
Karen at all. Many of them looked cross or sleepy, so
Karen told herself that it would be best not to try and
stop them. But Sue pushed her forward, hissing, "Say
hello. Get out there and meet them."

Karen forced herself to say hello to a few of them,
but she knew her voice wasn't forceful enough to make
them notice. Finally she was able to get one woman to
stop for a second. She said, "My name is Karen
Williams and I'm running for Queen in the Harvest
Parade. Will you vote for me?"

The woman frowned, shook her head, and said, "Haven't got any money." Then she walked off quickly, leaving Karen standing with a button in her hand and a lump in her throat.

During the next thirty minutes Karen was unable to get even one more person to stop and talk with her. By the time all the workers were in the store, Karen was so discouraged that she just wanted to turn around and go home. "Don't worry," Sue said. "The shoppers will be different."

Sue was right. At least, *some* of the shoppers were different. Some of them were almost friendly and they took the buttons that Sue and she handed out as they walked by. A few stopped to chat for a few minutes and Karen even knew one or two of them. But most of the shoppers were in a hurry and didn't seem to be the least bit interested in the Wilks County Harvest Queen Parade. The longer Karen stood out there on the shopping center parking lot, the more she felt like a fool.

The sun came out about ten thirty and it was clear the day was going to be a scorcher. By eleven one passer-by told them that it was already ninety degrees. "You got to be hot stuff to stand this, girlie."

Karen flushed even redder than the heat was making her. She'd already learned that some of the men would try to flirt with her or say things that would make her uncomfortable. One man had even tried to get her to leave her friends and go with him for a drink. Karen had declined quickly and looked around for Pete. Pete, though obviously not enjoying the day, was doing his best to keep them cheerful. Most of the time he read car magazines. About once an hour he would climb out of the little yellow and black Beetle that was parked beside the booth and go for Cokes. By noon Karen had consumed six cokes. She felt as though she might be sick, but she couldn't stop drinking. It was too hot.

"I wish Roger would get here," Karen said more than once. Though he'd agreed to help them, Roger had said he'd have to spend the morning at the dentist. He'd promised to get there by noon. It was already past that and Karen was getting impatient.

Roger drove up at exactly one o'clock. Karen was feeling very cross, very hot, very tired, and, most of all, she was beginning to lose hope that he would show. "Where have you been?" she asked angrily.

"The dentist kept me waiting for two hours. I didn't know they did things like that out here in the country. I thought they were only that sort of monsters in Chicago. Sorry." As Roger apologized, he opened his car door and swung his long legs out the door. "How's it going?"

It was all Karen could do to keep from wailing her troubles to him. Instead she managed a small grin and a short answer, "A little hot, a little depressing, but not bad."

"What do you mean not bad?" Sue demanded. "We've given almost all the flyers away and it's only one o'clock. I think we should go over to the copy center and get them to run off some more."

"We could pick up the ones on the ground," Karen said.

Sue flushed a dull, angry red. Karen hoped she could avert a scene by saying, "Sue, I was just kidding. You and Pete did a great job on the flyers. And the buttons are pure genius."

Looking mollified, Sue crossed her arms and said, "Well, I still think we should run off some more."

"We've already spent so much money," Karen objected. She seemed always to be the one who worried about money. She turned to Roger and asked, "Are you sure you're ready for this? The people passing by aren't exactly the best audience in the world. They hardly even notice me. In fact, a couple of times I've felt as though I were trying to sell refrigerators to Eskimos."

"Or sunlamps to Samoans?" Roger asked. Then he added, "You two looked bushed. Want me to go get some Cokes? Something to cool you off?"

Sue and Karen laughed together and Sue pointed to the paper bag that held empty Coke bottles. She said, "Thanks, but no thanks."

"How about lunch?" Roger asked. "Maybe you'd feel better if you had lunch."

"Do we look that bad?" Sue asked anxiously.

Karen felt her heart sink. If Sue became convinced that they looked grumpy and tired to Roger, she'd give Karen another lecture about putting on a good front. Karen wasn't sure she could stand any more of Sue's lectures. She turned to Roger and asked, "Who is your dentist?"

"His name is Dr. Watson," Roger answered. "I wanted to ask him about Sherlock, but I didn't dare. He had all those instruments of medieval torture on hand. I never crack corny jokes in the dentist's chair. Too terrifying." As Roger talked, he was tuning his guitar.

Karen asked, "Are you afraid of dentists?"

"Sure," Roger asked. "Isn't everyone?"

Karen was a little startled that Roger's answer was so prompt and honest. She had never heard a boy admit he was afraid so easily. In fact, she'd never heard a boy admit he was afraid. But, Karen reminded herself, she knew very little about men, really. She'd grown up in a household of women and her only opportunity to get to know boys was at school. At least in Wilks, boys and girls usually played separately. By junior high school, when they began to be interested in each other, they were also trying very hard to impress each other. Boys didn't tell the truth and neither did girls—at least, not all the truth.

But Roger didn't seem to be interested in impressing anyone. Were all the people in Chicago like him? she wondered. Then she blushed at the foolishness of the idea. Just because she'd grown up in a small town didn't mean that she was supposed to think like an idiot. She'd read enough and seen enough TV to know that Roger was very unusual for any place. Unusual but nice, Karen decided. For the first time it occurred to her that they might be friends—really good friends— the way she and Sue were.

Then Karen frowned. She had to be honest and admit that the friendship between Sue and her was becoming more and more strained as the contest campaign went on. It seemed to Karen that Sue was getting bossier and bossier, and Karen sometimes wanted to tell her to mind her own business. By the same token, Karen was pretty sure that Sue thought Karen was being impossible and letting everyone down. Karen sighed and touched the metal button pinned on her dress. Sue had gone to a lot of trouble to get these buttons made and Karen knew she should be grateful, but in truth she hated them. They made her feel silly.

"That's a big sigh," Roger said gently. "Why don't you sit down and let me sing you a song? Take a break, kiddo. You don't have to stand up all the time, do you?"

"Her dress will wrinkle," Sue said quickly. "I told her to buy nylon, not cotton."

Karen's fists clenched. For a second she felt as

though she were back in the kindergarten playground. She wanted to hit Sue just as hard as she could. Shamed by those thoughts, she tried to smooth things over. She said, "But I liked this color and cotton is cooler. Imagine how hot I'd be in a nylon dress."

"It wouldn't wrinkle," Sue said stubbornly.

Karen couldn't keep the scorn out of her voice. "That's true. The dress would look crisp no matter how much I wilted. Nothing matters but how things look, does it, Sue?"

"Well, the contest is based on looks," Sue answered reasonably. "Looks and personality. And the way you've been acting, you'd better hope it's based on looks."

"You don't like my personality?" Karen could hardly believe she was in the middle of this stupid argument. Her fists were still clenched and she felt like crying. But she couldn't stop taunting Sue. She felt as though she were completely out of control. She was sick of Sue's bossing, sick of Sue's acting as though Karen were a doll to be pushed around. She added, "You're the one who said I had to run because of my great personality. I didn't want to run, remember?"

"And I wish you hadn't!" Sue retorted. "If I'd known how awful you were going to act, I'd never have agreed to help you."

"Agreed to help me!" The anger and sarcasm in Karen's voice was thick now. "You didn't agree to help me. You took over from the very beginning. It's been your campaign right from the start."

"Wow!" Roger said. "You two really need a break. How about if we close up shop for a while and get some ice cream. Thirty minutes in an air-conditioned building will cool you off."

"I'll take Karen," Pete said. "Then you can take Sue later."

Karen hadn't even noticed that Pete was listening to the whole dreadful argument. She flushed with shame at the idea. Somehow it seemed much worse to have Pete hear how mean she'd been than to have Roger hear it. Karen smiled and said softly, "Sue, I'm sorry. I guess I'm just overheated."

There were tears in Sue's eyes. She held her lips in a firm line and said, "That's all right. I guess we're all hot and tired. But Pete's right. We can't all leave. You go with Pete and then I'll go later. Alone."

Karen felt awful when she heard the way Sue said, "Alone," and she said, "Let's all go together. It won't hurt to close up for a while."

"No," Sue said sharply. "Someone has to be here to mind the buttons and flyers. People might steal things."

"Why would anyone take things we're giving away?" Karen could not keep the edge out of her voice.

"Come on," Pete said quickly. "You and I will go now. Roger and Sue can go later. But the point is, let's go for a break."

Pete took her hand and led her away from the booth. As Karen walked with Pete, she resented the fact that he was taking her away without her permission. She felt just awful, but she tried to tell herself that she would feel better once she got inside the air-conditioned building.

Once inside, Karen began to shiver from the extreme change in temperature. She looked down at her bare arms and saw that there were goose bumps on her skin. She said to Pete, "Why do you think skin does that?"

"I don't know," Pete answered. It was clear that he wasn't interested in pursuing the subject.

Suddenly Karen felt a wave of anger wash over her. Why was it that Pete was so uninterested in so many things? All he really seemed to care about was cars and sports. Why wasn't he more like Roger? Roger would have talked for half an hour on the subject of goose bumps—or any other subject that came to mind.

Karen looked at her tall, blond boyfriend who sat beside her on the counter. His head was bent and he was deeply engrossed in reading the menu. Did she really love Pete? Or was that just an idea that had been pushed on her by Sue and the others? Confused by the sudden turn of her thoughts, Karen shook her head and wiped her damp forehead with a paper napkin. No doubt about it, the heat was making her cross and confused and maybe even a little crazy. "I hate hot weather," she said.

"Better than winter," Pete said reasonably. "Think how hard it would be to campaign in a blizzard."

"The way I feel today, I'd make a better candidate for Snow Queen than anything else." But even as she talked, she realized that Pete wouldn't have any idea that she was referring to the evil Snow Queen in Andersen's fairy tales. She doubted that Pete had ever even heard of Hans Christian Andersen.

Karen sighed and ordered a glass of lemonade. Pete asked, "Don't you want a sandwich or something?"

"No thanks," Karen said. "I'm too hot."

"You haven't had anything at all today but Cokes," Pete reminded her gently.

By the tone of his voice Karen knew that Pete was afraid to cross her. She tried to answer without sounding angry. "I'm not hungry, Pete. I'm not going to eat."

He said nothing more. They drank their lemonades and Pete had a tuna fish sandwich. He ate quietly, not talking much, and Karen was glad of that. It was good to be out of the heat for a while and it was good to be away from Sue's constant nagging. She still felt awful, but at least this was a small break in the day. When Pete picked up the check and walked to the cash register, Karen followed him quietly.

Over the cash register a clock said two o'clock. Karen sighed and said, "You mean I have to stand out there for another eight hours?"

Pete pretended he didn't hear her and that made Karen very angry. She was almost as upset when she went back to the booth as she had been before her lemonade break. It didn't help when Sue said, "I'm glad you're back. A lot of people came by looking for you."

"Who were they?" Karen asked.

"How do I know?" Sue answered. "Just people who asked where you were."

"I tried to get Sue to masquerade as you, but she said she'd rather be herself," Roger said.

Karen knew Roger was trying to be funny, but Sue apparently thought he was making fun of her. She turned to him and frowned. Then she turned back to Karen and said, "You should have repaired your face while you were there. Now you'll have to use the mirror in the car again."

"You make me sound like a broken down car or something. 'Repair your face.'" Karen grumbled. But she dutifully went to the car to use the makeup kit her mother and sister had packed for her. By the time she had her mascara and eyeliner replaced, Sue was walking away with Roger.

Karen watched the two of them walk through the parking lot toward the ice cream shop. Sue looked short and a little dumpy beside Roger's tall, lanky body. No doubt about it, Roger would need a taller girlfriend. Not that Roger and Sue would ever be interested in each other anyway. No. Roger would need a more unusual girl—one who shared his interests in music and books, one with more curiosity about life. Someone more like me? Karen asked herself.

She shook her head, almost ruining the line she was painting on her mouth with the coral color. All this heat was making her crazier than usual. She wasn't interested in Roger and neither was Sue. She was dating Pete and Sue was dating John. That was the way it was and that was the way it was supposed to be. Roger wasn't even important in their world. Roger was someone who might not even be a friend when school started. Roger was very, very different from their crowd.

She smiled falsely at herself in the mirror, willing herself to look pretty and pleasant. But the lovely young teenager who smiled back seemed like a ghost. Who was that sweet young girl with the bright smile and lovely hair? And how was it that the heat only made her hot cheeks rosier and her auburn hair curlier? Why didn't her reflection reflect the miserable mood she was in? Was she just imagining her problems? Or was she really as phony and shallow as people seemed to want her to be?

Karen shivered and climbed out of the car. She walked back into the parking lot, feeling the blacktop beneath her feet as a sticky mess that seemed to sink down with her weight. The sun was gone now and the day was overcast. Her premonitions of the morning had turned out to be correct. It was a gloomy and terrible day after all. You could see it even in the faces of the shoppers who passed by her booth.

She forced herself to smile cheerfully and handed her flyers to everyone who passed by. She chatted with those who would stop to talk, asking them to vote for her. She gossiped comfortably about babies, new houses, and marriages to those few people she knew as friends and acquaintances of her or her family. She was constantly surprised at how many people remembered her mother and sister as Harvest Queens of years past. Karen was sure that if she did win the contest it would be in large measure because of fond memories of her mother and sister. And why not? They were both lovely women—just the sort of woman she hoped to grow up to be. But, Karen told herself honestly, she had a long, long way to go. Especially when she was in a mood as black as this one.

But even as she thought gratefully of her mother and sister, her mood got darker. They were nice women, and pretty too. But what had it got them? Were they happy? Karen didn't think they were very happy and neither was she. If being Queen of the Harvest Parade hadn't made them happy, then how would it help her?

"It is hot," said Roger when he and Sue returned. "Do you think it's going to rain?"

"Can't rain," Sue said. "The forecast said clear skies."

"Can the sky read?" Roger asked.

No one laughed. He looked from one of them to the other. Sue was the most bedraggled-looking one of all. Her T-shirt and hair both clung to her sturdy body as though pasted. Pete was still curled up in the car reading magazines and drinking Cokes. He looked as though he might go to sleep any minute. Only Karen looked as though she were holding up well. He smiled at her and asked, "How do you manage it? You look as crisp as the celery I pulled this morning. What do you use? Magic?"

Instead of the smile he expected, he saw a displeased

look on Karen's face. She answered sharply, "I use voodoo. You know, voodoo is the black magic of beauty queens."

Roger laughed softly and answered, "Hard to imagine you using black magic. You're the nicest person I know."

Karen turned her back to him deliberately and waved to a woman who was walking about twenty feet away. She called out in what she hoped was a cheerful voice, "Mrs. Simmons. Over here. Don't your kids want a button?"

Mrs. Simmons, looking very hot and tired, with her four children in tow, changed her course and came over to the booth where Karen was handing out the flyers. She stood politely while Karen pinned a button on each of the little ones. When she was finished, Mrs. Simmons said, "I'll vote for you if I can remember. I'm too busy to read the paper these days. My dad's sick and I have the kids to tend."

"That's fine," Karen said. "Anyway, the kids seem to like the buttons."

The minute Mrs. Simmons and her brood were gone, Sue said crossly, "Don't give any more buttons to kids. We're running low."

"The kids may be your best supporters," Roger said.

Sue glared at him and snapped, "You're supposed to play music, not run the campaign. I'm the one who paid for the buttons."

"But you're not the one running for queen," Roger said softly.

Before Sue could reply, Pete climbed out of the car, stretched his arms, and yawned. He said, "Sue's right. The buttons should go to people who can vote."

"The buttons should go to whomever Karen wants to

give them to," Roger said. Again his voice was very quiet.

"Says who?" Pete said nastily. "Just sing, city boy. I'm the campaign manager, not you."

"Don't make fun of me for being different," Roger said. "It displays your ignorance."

Karen looked from one fellow to the other. She was dismayed that a simple argument between Sue and her over campaign buttons could have flared into open warfare between the two boys so quickly. She said, "Don't argue. Please." Her voice was more of a cry than a request.

She put one hand on Pete's arm, looking up at him with a soft plea in her eyes. "Pete," she said, "I just want us to all be friends. All we've done all day is fight."

Sue made a funny little sound in her throat and Karen knew that Sue was trying to say that it was she, Karen, who'd been doing most of the fighting. But arguing with Sue was an old pattern from childhood. It wasn't frightening the way this argument between Pete and Roger was frightening. She couldn't bear to have them fight with each other. It would be too horrible.

Pete was standing with clenched fists, legs outspread as though he were ready to fight. Roger was facing him, his body tense but his fists unclenched.

Roger said, "I think you and Sue should listen to Karen once in a while. She knows what she's doing."

"What I'd like to know is what you think you're doing?" Pete answered.

Karen felt like a fool standing between the two guys, trying desperately to think of something to say that would stop a fight that seemed now to be inevitable. The only words she could think of were, "Please . . ."

Fortunately, just then, the sky opened up and rain started to pour down on them. Lightning flashed, thunder cracked, and a high wind began to blow. Flyers flew off the table and onto the parking lot floor.

Sue cried, "Get the flyers. They're getting ruined!"

Roger and Pete dropped their militant poses and ran to help Sue rescue the flyers. Karen stood stiffly, watching the three of them work to salvage their equipment. They all seemed to have forgotten she existed.

Water rolled from the heavens onto her warm body, draining off the heat. For the first time all day, Karen felt somewhat comfortable. Her heartbeat slowed and her pulse returned to normal. She had been saved. She could go home now. No one would expect her to stand out here in this downpour looking like a drowned rat. No one would expect her to campaign in the rain.

She turned and walked away from the busy scene in front of her. She wasn't needed to help clean up the mess. She was only needed to look pretty. And how could she look pretty in the rain?

Someone called to her. She wasn't sure who it was. She kept right on walking. As far as she could tell, she was free for the time being. No one needed her at the moment.

10

Without really realizing what she was doing, Karen walked through the parking lot, onto the highway, and down the road until she came to the street that turned off to the river. The rain was now coming down in torrents, making it difficult to see and even harder to walk. Her yellow canvas shoes with the rope soles squished and slid in the deep water that rushed across the sidewalk.

At one point it became difficult to walk and Karen bent over long enough to pull off the shoes. The thought of turning around or seeking shelter never occurred to her. She walked on against the driving wind that blew the rain toward her, drenching her from top to toe. She wasn't thinking about Pete or Sue or Roger or what they would think when they discovered she was missing. She thought only of forcing her way forward against the wind and rain.

In a way, the water felt good. Her body was cooler now, and the wetness seemed almost like a caress, trickling down her face to her shoulders and down the open neck of her yellow dress. Now that she was barefoot, it was easy to walk and the water felt good on her tired feet.

As she neared the river's edge, she watched the willow trees dance in the wind. Lightning crackled and thunder roared about her ears. Karen wondered briefly if it would be safe to sit under the trees.

She was ready for shelter now and ran toward a large old willow tree near the edge of the river. She seated herself on a fallen log and leaned against the rough bark of the old tree. Leaning her head back, she closed her eyes and let the tears run down her face. It was a relief to sob her heart out here in this dark, deserted, and damp spot. No one could hear her. No one could tell her to smile. No one could tell her she was a lucky girl. She could feel just as sorry for herself as she wanted to.

The storm raged for another few minutes and then, as quickly as it came, it disappeared. Karen didn't open her eyes, but she felt the sun come out, and beyond the occasional drips from the old willow tree the air was dry.

Suddenly she heard Roger's voice ask softly, "You all through crying?"

Karen opened her eyes and sat up straight. Roger was crouched in front of her, holding out a wet handkerchief. He smiled and said, "I'm not sure it will help, but it's the best I can do."

"You're all wet," Karen said. "You look . . ."

"Like a drowned chipmunk?" Roger asked hopefully. "Or maybe a nice squirrel? I'd hate to have you think of me as a rat."

Karen laughed and asked, "How long have you been there?"

"I followed you," Roger admitted. "I hope you don't mind, but you seemed in sort of a daze. Are you really that upset about being in this contest, Karen?"

"Where are Pete and Sue?" Karen asked quickly. She wouldn't be able to bear it if they came here and dragged her back to the parking lot. Then she reminded herself that they wouldn't want her to show herself at all, looking like this. She said in the next breath, "I bet I look awful."

"Sort of," Roger said, and then he grinned. "But I bet if you used this handkerchief to wipe off the mascara that's dripping off the end of your nose, you'd look just fine."

Karen took the handkerchief quickly and scrubbed her face briskly. Then she asked, "All gone?"

"All gone," Roger said.

"Pete and Sue?" Karen asked again.

Roger grinned. "I'm afraid I sent them in the wrong direction. It should be at least thirty minutes before they figure out they are on a wild goose chase. By then you will have had time to explain to me exactly why you're in a contest that you so obviously despise."

"Does it show that much?" Karen asked.

Roger nodded and explained, "I've always known you were not the typical beauty queen. Anyone can see you're much too sensible to let things like that rule your life. But until today I figured it was something you wanted to do. You looked as though you were having fun. You always looked happy."

Tears began rolling down Karen's cheeks again. Deep sobs, which she couldn't control, seemed to well up from her chest. Roger waited for her to finish. Finally, he said, "Want to talk about it?"

"From as far back as I can remember," Karen began, "they all expected me to be Harvest Queen. It wasn't anything anyone ever asked me if I wanted to do. It was just there. My mother and my sister were queens, so naturally I had to be one, too. No one ever asked me if I wanted to do it."

Roger's handkerchief was too wet to be any help, so Karen lifted the edge of her full skirt and wiped her eyes as she continued talking. "So I guess until it happened, I never really thought about whether or not I wanted it. It just seemed like something I was *supposed* to want. Do you see what I mean?"

Roger nodded his head. "I have friends who go to college just because their parents expect them to. It doesn't usually work too well. And now this isn't working for you. Can't you quit?"

"Quit?" Karen asked. "But everyone expects me to win. How could I disappoint them?"

"Isn't it better to disappoint other people than to disappoint yourself?" Roger asked.

Karen studied him carefully, searching for the answers to his question. As she looked at him, she found herself drawing closer and closer to his soft gray eyes. It seemed as though, somehow, if she could just get close enough, she could find the answer to his question there.

As she stretched toward him, she raised one hand and put it on his arm, pulling him to her. Then, tilting her head, she moved her lips toward his.

Roger put his arms around her shoulder, drawing her close to him, responding quickly and warmly to her kiss. Kissing Roger was a lot like falling into a soft, deep bed of flowers. Never, never had she felt like this. She could feel his heart beating quickly through the damp white shirt that he was wearing.

Finally, he pulled away. In a deep voice, with his hands still holding her shoulders tightly, he said, "But this isn't solving your problem, is it?"

"Isn't it?" Karen asked, and for the first time all day she felt glad to be alive. She pulled back from Roger and sighed. "I think I could quit. My mom and sister will be disappointed, but it's probably the best thing to do. Why should I be queen when all the other girls want it so much? I don't really deserve it."

"Don't quit for other girls. Don't do that to yourself," Roger warned. "If you quit, quit because you want to."

"Well, I've found out, thanks to you, that I really do want to quit. And I want to thank you, Roger. You've made me understand that I should. And with your help I'll be able to face everybody."

Roger shook his head slowly. His face looked very serious as he pulled her close to him again, pressing his lips against her soft auburn hair. He whispered in her ear, "Karen, you're a wonderful girl, but you still haven't got my message, have you? Don't quit the contest for others. Don't quit the contest for me. And don't quit the contest hoping that I'll make it up to you somehow. Whatever you do, you'll have to do on your own. Don't count on me to make it easier for you."

Karen felt as though he had slapped her in the face. She drew back quickly, her face white with shock. She said in a strangled voice, "I wasn't counting on you, Roger Micklovich. How could I count on you? You don't even belong here."

With that, she stood up abruptly and ran up the path to the highway. She didn't turn to see if Roger was behind her until she got to the top of the hill. Then she turned quickly. Out of the corner of her eye, she could see Roger still sitting on the fallen log. He hadn't moved.

11

When she got home, they were all waiting for her. Sue, Lucy, her mother, and Pete sat around the kitchen table with cold drinks in front of them. She could tell that she had interrupted a conversation, and from their self-conscious looks she could tell that it had been about her.

"Hi, Honey," her mother said, trying to keep her voice light. "Are you hungry? We thought we might all go out for pizza. Sound all right to you?"

"Sure," she said. "Are you ready to go?"

"We've been waiting for you," Sue said. There was a note of criticism in her voice.

Realizing that they'd all decided the best way to handle things was to ignore the fact that she'd run away, Karen decided that she might as well fall in with their plan. She said, "I'm a bit bedraggled, but I can be ready in about twenty minutes." She looked down at her wrinkled cotton dress and yellow canvas shoes that looked as though they'd never come clean and added, "I walked down to the river and I guess I got kind of wet."

None of the others responded and Karen realized they were determined not to talk about her abrupt departure. She winced as she imagined how tough that probably was for them. Were they just trying to be nice or were they afraid to hear what she had to say?

Deciding that the best thing to do was nothing, at least until she'd had time to think, Karen smiled at them and said, "I'll be right back." She went into the bedroom she shared with Lucy to find some other clothes. A shower, a few minutes with the blow dryer, and new makeup would only take about twenty minutes. She selected her best-fitting Levis and a pretty cotton print shirt with flowers on it.

Frowning at the yellow shoes on her closet floor, Karen wondered if they were ruined. If so, she would have to wear her white sandals with the dress after this. She absolutely was not going to let her mother spend any more money on clothes for her.

As she showered and dried her hair, Karen went over her encounter with Roger that afternoon. At first, all she could think of was his cold refusal to help her. How could he reject her so quickly? Perhaps, Karen thought, perhaps Roger had never been interested in her at all. In that case, he must have thought that she was terrible when she'd leaned over to kiss him. But would he have kissed her so warmly if he had not been interested in her at all? Somehow that didn't fit with anything she knew about Roger. He just wasn't that kind of boy. Man, she corrected herself. Roger was a young man, not a boy.

Why, oh, why? she asked herself. Why had he changed so abruptly? How could he have been so cruel? Why did he say she couldn't count on him? Didn't she mean anything at all to him?

As her troubled thoughts ran round and round, another part of her was remembering the shared kisses. Each time she thought of those kisses, she felt little goose bumps on her arms and a rush of excitement ran through her body. Kissing Roger had been a wonderful experience for her. Roger had stirred her in a way that no other boy had. Kissing Roger was very, very different from anything she'd ever experienced before.

A tear fell from Karen's left eye as she worked the soft fluffy strokes of her brow pen on her right eyebrow. She blinked and two tears fell from her right eye. Before she could control it, soft tears of memory rolled down her newly madeup face. She reached for Kleenex and remembered Roger's damp handkerchief. The thought of his wonderful smile as he'd offered the handkerchief brought fresh tears.

She wiped her eyes with a hot towel, sighing because she would have to redo her eye makeup. Then someone rapped sharply on the bathroom door. Karen's heart leaped and her pulse raced. "Yes?" she called.

"Karen," Lucy said, "we're all waiting for you."

"You want me to look right, don't you?" Karen could hear the anger and disappointment in her retort. She admitted to herself that she had been hoping that Lucy would tell her that Roger was on the phone.

Karen drew a sharp breath and vowed to take hold of herself. She was not going to wait around hoping that Roger would call. No. She was not ever going to be the sort of female who whined and cried for her true love to call. It was clear enough that Roger wasn't interested in pursuing their brief encounter. She didn't have to be a genius to figure that out.

Despite her resolution, Karen had a hard time keeping a cheerful face during dinner. Several times people stopped by their table at the pizza hut to wish her luck in the contest. A couple of them even mentioned seeing her in the shopping center earlier in the day. One man said, "I think you have stamina, young lady. It was a really tough day and you stuck it out. Stamina and good looks. That's an unbeatable combination." Then he paused and broke into laughter at his own joke, "Too bad you're not a racehorse. I'd sure put my two dollars on you."

Karen tried to smile politely, but she wasn't sure she really liked being compared to a racehorse. When he left, Sue said, "See? I told you that campaigning in the shopping center would help. I told you so. . . ." Her voice trailed off and her face flushed. She looked very embarrassed.

Karen laughed out loud at her friend's obvious despair at breaking her apparent agreement with the others. Between laughs, she said, "That's okay, Sue. You can talk about the campaign if you want to. I won't run off twice in the same day. One dramatic exit a day, that's my motto."

Even as she said this, Karen felt her heart sink. Hadn't she just made it a lot harder for herself to quit the campaign as she had decided to do? She took another bite of pizza and said, "But I guess I should tell you that I'm thinking of dropping out of the campaign."

Her mother's face went ashen gray, now Karen wished she had not spoken. After all, why worry her mother needlessly? Still, she couldn't pretend that everything was all right when it wasn't. She turned to her mother and added, "Of course, I don't think I really will."

Her mother tried to smile as she said, "No one wants to force you into anything. I just heard from Lucy this afternoon that I forced her into running. After all these years, she tells me that . . ."

"Mama," Lucy interrupted. "I'm sorry you misunderstood what I was saying so completely. I want to talk to you about it some more, but not now. We agreed that tonight we'd talk about other things."

"That's what I hate the most," her mother complained. "I just don't understand how all of a sudden we can't talk about things. We never used to keep secrets. At least, I never thought we did." With this, she looked at Lucy with a sad expression.

"If you don't listen, I can't explain," Lucy said in an angry voice. She crumpled her napkin and put it on the table.

Sue asked, "Anyone want that last piece of pizza?"

"Not me," Pete said. "I've got to go to the gas station. I work till midnight tonight." He turned to Karen and said, "What time do you want to go tomorrow?"

"Go?" Karen asked. She had no idea what he was talking about.

"Go to the city to pick up the parts. You said you'd ride with me."

Was she wrong or was there a note of anger in Pete's voice too? Suddenly Karen was very, very tired of people and the problems that people seemed to bring. She said, "I think I'll skip tomorrow. I think I'll stay home and read all day. I need the rest."

"I could use some help on the farm," Sue said. "If you're not going to campaign, you could help me."

Karen passed a hand over her forehead and said,

"I'm so tired. I have a headache. I might be getting sick. I'm going to stay home." Even as she spoke, she felt like a coward. Why couldn't she just have told Sue the truth? Why did she have to pretend to be sick? She didn't have to help Sue on the farm just because Sue expected it. What did Sue ever do for her?

Maybe I am sick, Karen thought. She certainly was very confused and mixed up to be thinking that way about Sue. Her friend did a lot for her. Why, Sue had done more for the campaign than anyone. Sue was the best help she'd had.

But Karen couldn't find it in her heart to express her gratitude to Sue. Nor could she find the words to explain to anyone else exactly how she felt. Describing herself as sick seemed the easiest and most accurate thing she could do.

Pete left them, looking hurt because Karen wouldn't be going with him tomorrow. Karen wondered if he were jealous. It wasn't like Pete to allow himself to get into such a fierce argument as he'd had with Roger.

"It's so hot today," Karen said. "I think it's made us all a little crazy."

"How about a nice air-conditioned movie?" Lucy suggested.

"We've seen it," her mother protested.

"We could drive to Redding for the second feature," Lucy suggested. "The ride would do us good."

"The gas is too expensive," Karen and her mother said in one breath.

"Well, at least we agree on *one* thing today," said Mrs. Williams.

Karen felt guilty, and flushed. She said, "Let's just go home and forget about it."

"I was just trying to think of some place air-conditioned," Lucy explained. "The apartment is like an oven."

But in the end they went home to their apartment. Karen read, her mother watched television, and Lucy washed her hair and did her nails. They all went to bed early. Karen didn't go to sleep until almost three o'clock in the morning. It was not only the heat—she couldn't stop thinking about Roger. Where had she gone wrong?

When she woke the next morning, Karen was determined to quit the contest. She spent the day reading and waiting for her mother to come home from work. What she didn't want to admit to herself was that she also spent the day waiting for Roger to call. By evening she was so sick at heart because neither Roger nor Pete had called her that she couldn't bear to get into another wrangle with her mother.

She and her mother talked about a lot of things during dinner, but neither of them mentioned the contest. Karen was glad that she wasn't actually scheduled to go anywhere for the next three nights. It was the middle of August now, and in August most of the local organizations canceled their usual meetings. Not only were a lot of people on vacation, but most of the people connected to farming were too busy with the harvests to do anything but work. The parade on Labor Day was the signal that summer was officially over and people could go back to their usual pace of life.

The next day, Karen decided that she would call Roger and tell him how she felt. She wanted desperately to explain why it would be easier to drop out of the contest if he would stand by her. She tried hundreds of different combinations of words to let him know how much his friendship meant to her. But though she went to the phone three times, she did not pick it up to dial his number. There was simply no way to explain that she needed to feel that he cared about her. Besides, she was afraid that Roger really didn't care about her. She would hate to make a bigger fool of herself than she already had.

"If he wants me, he'll call," Karen told herself. But he didn't call, despite the fact that she turned down invitations from Sue and Pete in order to be home, close to the telephone. Karen acknowledged her anger and grief that night, and instead of worrying about Roger she promised herself she would put him out of her mind completely.

When he didn't call on Wednesday or Thursday, she was sure he never would. But by then she was feeling stronger. She was able to get through the days without breaking into tears or falling into long silences while she thought about the times that she and Roger had shared. Yet when the telephone rang, her heart raced as though she were a champion skiier on the downhill slope.

It was never Roger. As the week wore on, Karen became more and more resigned to the fact that Roger wasn't going to call. But it wasn't just Roger that kept her lying awake at night. She was also terribly worried as she tried to make up her mind about the contest. Did she dare drop out of the Harvest Parade? How could she possibly disappoint Lucy and her mother in that way? What could she ever say that would explain to them how she felt?

Each morning she rose with the complete determination to resign from the contest. But each morning her resolution faded as she greeted her mother. Finally, on Friday, she admitted to herself that she absolutely could not bear to disappoint her mother in that cruel way. No, she was in the contest and she was going to stay. If Roger was sure she should drop out, that was only his opinion. She was just as sure that she should avoid hurting her mother. After all, keeping a promise was just as important as being honest with yourself. Wasn't it?

12

When she finally decided that she was definitely going to stay in the contest, Karen felt better than she'd felt all week. That Friday evening she was able to talk with her mother and sister without feeling as though there were a great wall between them. Though Roger hadn't called her all week, Karen tried to act cheerful as they drove out to the Women's Club meeting, where Karen would be appearing with the other contestants.

"Now try and look as though you really want to win," Sue warned as they walked toward the Women's Club building.

Karen turned to her friend and said, "Sue, I know you mean to be helpful, but I want you to stop giving me advice. I promise you, from now on I'm going to work just as hard as I can to win the contest. Now I want you to promise me not to be so bossy."

Sue flushed and frowned, then she muttered, "I was only trying to help."

"I know you were," Karen said calmly. "But the point is, you're not really helping me at all. In fact, your constant advice only makes me angry and nervous."

Sue opened her mouth, looking as though she wanted to answer Karen's criticism with some angry words of her own, but she didn't. Instead she said, "You know, you've changed Karen. You're not as nice as you used to be. You aren't so great that you don't need friends, you know."

"I need friends, and I hope you are one," Karen answered. Her face was flushing with excitement and her heart was racing as it always did when she and Sue got into an argument. She was very aware that she and Sue were standing on the edge of the parking lot beside the Women's Club building. She knew that Lucy and her mother could hear the conversation and she was afraid that other people might be able to also. But Karen was determined to make her position very clear to her friend. As she'd lain awake nights, worrying what to do, it had become apparent to her that Sue was making her miserable about the contest.

"If you are my friend," Karen continued, "you'll want to be helpful. The best help you can give me between now and voting day is to stop giving me warnings and advice. It makes me feel as though I'm doing a bad job as a contestant. It makes me feel bad about myself."

"You *are* doing a bad job," Sue said angrily. "You are only doing what you absolutely have to. You're going to lose if you don't watch out."

Karen could hear her mother and sister draw in their

121

breaths sharply. She knew that she would have to speak quickly or they would jump to her defense. Her mother would never be able to tolerate anyone criticizing her daughter, but Karen wanted to make sure that this time she fought her own battle. "I'm not going to lose," she said. "Thank you for all your help. I hope you'll continue to help me. But from now on I'm doing the planning myself." Then she turned to her mother and sister and smiled, "With your help, of course. You make me feel good about myself, not bad."

Sue said, "You're going to lose," and with that she started walking away from them.

Karen was pretty sure that Sue was crying. She was sorry, but she didn't call out to her friend to come back. Karen knew she had to take charge of her campaign herself.

Lucy smiled quickly at Karen and made a victory sign with her two fingers. She said, "Good for you, Tiger. I've been waiting for you to do that for years. I'll drive her home."

"Try to explain to her," Karen asked softly. There were tears in her eyes as she watched Lucy chase after Sue and persuade her to get into the car. But underneath the tears, Karen felt a certain relief and pride about finally standing up to Sue.

Her mother said, "I never did like that girl. She was always bossing you around."

Karen shook her head gently and took her mother's hand. "Don't talk that way about Sue. She'll probably be back at our kitchen table by tomorrow night. I just hope that she understands that I meant what I said about running the campaign my way."

Her mother looked at her anxiously and asked, "Karen, do you really want to drop out?"

"No, Mama. I thought maybe I did want to drop out, but I've decided that what I really want to do is win. I want to make you and Lucy proud of me."

Her mother squeezed her hand and said, "I've always been proud of you. You know that it doesn't matter whether you win or lose, don't you? I love you no matter what. It's just that . . ."

"It's just that you wanted me to be happy," Karen finished for her. "I understand that, Mama. And I want you to be happy. And we will be happy—either way. But I'm going to try really hard to win, Mama. You'll see." Karen leaned over and kissed her mother on the cheek. She really did feel better about being in the contest than she ever had. Now that she realized that pleasing her mother was what she wanted to do, she was happy with her decision. Or at least she would be happy, if she could stop thinking about Roger.

Roger wouldn't understand her decision at all. She was sure that once her decision to stay in the contest was made she'd forfeited any chance she'd ever had to gain Roger's love. Karen sighed and told herself that she couldn't help that. She'd made the choice that she thought was right and that was all she could do. If Roger thought the Harvest Queen contest was corny and stupid, that was just too bad. She wasn't going to disappoint her mother by dropping out in the middle of the contest.

Karen walked into the Women's Club building holding her mother's hand. It felt good to know exactly what she was going to do. It seemed to Karen that she'd spent most of the summer going back and forth in her mind about how to handle her feelings and how to

please other people. That was a lot of the trouble,
Karen knew now. She'd been trying too hard to please
others, just the way Roger had said. But what Roger
would never understand was that she wanted to please
others. That was who she was.

Laughing at herself for her complicated thinking,
Karen walked up to the other contestants and smiled as
she said a friendly hello. Then she sat down in the
empty chair beside Charlotte Melville and waited for
the program to begin. This was one of the few times
when she would appear simultaneously with the other
contestants. She was interested to hear them and
not very nervous about her own speech. It would be
short and by now she was used to speaking before
groups.

Charlotte leaned over and whispered, "How was the
shopping center last Saturday?"

"Grim," Karen said. "It rained."

"I'll be there tomorrow," Charlotte said.

"Good," Karen said. "It will be more fun."

"You don't mind?" Charlotte asked. "It was your
idea. Or, at least, you did it first."

"I don't mind," Karen assured the other girl. "How's
it going door to door?"

Charlotte shrugged.

"I'm going to do that next week," Karen said.

"I thought you didn't want to go door to door?"
Charlotte said.

"I didn't," Karen admitted. "But I've changed my
mind."

The program began then and the contestants didn't
dare do anything but sit quietly, looking just as interested as they could manage, while a botanist from the
neighboring university spoke about the joys of breeding

your own hybrid flowers. Actually, Karen found the woman's talk interesting because she was interested in gardening, but she was sure that most of the audience was bored. There was much foot shuffling and paper rattling.

When it was time to introduce the contestants, many of the people in the audience looked restless. Karen watched their faces as each of the girls went to the podium and delivered her prepared speech. Though they obviously felt friendly toward the girls, Karen could see that the restless behavior returned when a girl talked more than a minute or two. Louisa May Martin talked too long and so did Lois Welschmire. By the time Sarah Weintraub stood up to speak several people were standing up and stretching. Karen felt her nervousness grow as she reviewed her prepared speech. Was it too long?

Finally, her name was called and she went to the front of the room. She began her speech by praising the Women's Club, the speaker, Wilks County, and Kansas. Then she skipped all the way to the center of the speech, leaving out how much she wanted to win and what a deserving candidate she was. Instead she said, "I'm not going to talk long because you've been very patient. Just let me say that if I'm elected I will be following a tradition set by two other Williams women, my mother and my sister. I always wanted to be like them because I think they are fine women. That's the real reason I became a contestant, and that's the real reason I want to win. Thank you."

As Karen sat down, she thought her applause seemed longer and louder than for the other contestants. At least, she hoped so. She made it her business to get around and talk with as many people as she could during the serving of coffee and refreshments. In general, campaigning seemed easier than it ever had before. About ten o'clock she found herself looking at the door, wondering if Pete would come to pick her up. But she wasn't as anxious as she'd been in the past to escape the crowd. When Pete didn't come, she wasn't surprised. She hadn't been very nice to Pete this week. In fact, she'd turned down three offers he'd made for dates. Perhaps he was finished with her also.

Roger. Sue. Pete. Karen couldn't help think that she'd miss them all. But she was determined not to let that sadness keep her from doing her very best at campaigning tonight. And tomorrow she would be out there in that shopping center, even if she had to campaign alone.

On the way home from the Women's Club meeting, Lucy asked, "What time will Pete and Roger set up the booth tomorrow?"

"I'm not sure if Pete will be there," Karen said. "I'm positive that Roger won't."

"Are you sure?" Lucy asked.

"No, I'm not sure," Karen admitted. "We talked last week about all of us putting the booth up at ten thirty. We decided that getting there before the shopping center opened was silly. But I haven't heard from Roger all week and Pete is probably mad at me, too."

"Does that too mean in addition to Roger or Sue?" Lucy asked. "Or don't you want to talk about it?"

"I don't know what to say," Karen answered. "I guess the best thing is to go to the shopping center tomorrow and see who shows up."

"I'll be there," her mother said.

"So will I," Lucy added.

"Then everything will be fine," Karen said. But in her heart she knew that nothing would be fine unless Roger was there. Yet she was almost sure that Roger wouldn't be there. Of course, she couldn't help but hope. It was all right to dream, wasn't it?

13

Karen saw Pete first. His bright yellow hair gleamed in the morning sunshine as he bent to pull the booth posts into position. It was a minute before Karen realized that Sue and Roger were helping him.

She was so happy that she almost skipped over to them, saying quickly, "How wonderful to see you all. Hi, Sue, Pete, Roger." Her heart skipped a beat and her voice faltered as she spoke Roger's name. He looked up from his struggles with the posts and grinned at her, saying, "I heard you were still in the running."

"Yes," Karen said. And she couldn't help but wonder if he was going to say something disapproving.

But the boys were struggling too hard to put the booth together to say anything. Karen ran over to help them lift the counter into place. "Watch out!" Sue warned, and then she clapped her hand over her mouth.

"I won't get dirty," Karen said. "It took too long to get the mud out of this dress to risk a second grimy experience." She laughed and stepped back, looking with an admiring expression at the big sign they were stapling between the two posts. It said, KAREN WILLIAMS FOR QUEEN.

"I hope you like it," Sue said anxiously. "I wouldn't have brought it, but I'd already made it and it seemed a shame not to use it." She waited hesitantly for Karen to approve of her work.

Karen smiled and said, "It's a great sign, Sue. Thank you."

Sue said, "Okay. I'm glad you like it. See you later."

"Where are you going?" Pete asked. He seemed very surprised that Sue was leaving.

"I'm going to spend the day with John," Sue said. "We're going to the lake and who knows what else." She smiled a brief, sad smile at Karen and added, "And I'm sorry about last night."

"Stay," Karen said. "We can use the help."

But Sue shook her head and said, "You have plenty of help. And I've got better things to do." With that, she turned and walked away.

Karen looked at the back of her friend retreat across the parking lot and she felt a great sadness. It was like watching some part of herself walk away. She realized that Sue was hurt and she was sorry about that. But Karen also knew that she had been right. Sue had been too critical and too bossy. It would be easier to campaign without her—as soon as the lump in her throat dissolved.

She swallowed and looked at Pete and Roger, asking, "Are you two leaving also?"

"No," Pete said. He seemed as bewildered by the question as by Sue's retreat. He asked, "You two have another fight?"

Karen realized that he didn't understand any of the struggles she'd been having about the contest. If that was true, then he probably didn't know how happy and excited she'd been to discover that he and Roger were putting up the booth. Pete seemed to have missed a lot of the emotional tension in the air and Karen was grateful for that. She answered quickly, "I think she might be a little angry at me. But she'll get over it." Even if she didn't really believe that, it seemed the best thing to say. Then she smiled and said, "But look at all the wonderful help that I have. Mama and Lucy, you and Roger. It's going to be a wonderful day."

Before Pete could ask her any more questions about her quarrel with Sue, she spied a couple getting out of their car. "Hello there," Karen called. "Wait just a minute, will you?" Then she walked swiftly over to where they were standing and held out a flyer. "I'm Karen Williams . . ." she began.

By the time she'd talked with the couple for a while, then returned to the booth, Lucy and Roger were gone. "Where are they?" Karen asked. She hoped her voice didn't betray her fear that they'd abandoned her after all.

"Lucy went for coffee," her mother explained. "I think Roger went home for a little while."

"Where did Roger go?" Karen demanded of Pete.

Pete shrugged and answered, "He said he had a date. I think he'll be back later."

Karen felt her heart sink with disappointment. So Roger hadn't really forgiven her at all? She was sure he'd only come this morning to keep his promise. It would be like Roger to remember that he'd said he'd help Pete put up the booth no matter how disinterested he was in the contest or Karen.

She clenched her fists in frustration, fighting back the need to scream or to cry out in rage and disappointment. She tried to tell herself that she was very, very angry at Roger for running out on her like that. And what did Pete mean that he had a date? How could he have a date with some other girl after the way he'd kissed her?

Her face flushed with shame as she remembered that those wonderful shared kisses had been her idea, not his. No. From the very first she'd made a fool of herself over Roger, but she wouldn't do that again. From now on she was going to pay all her attention to Pete. Pete was the one who was really her boyfriend. It was Pete who loved her.

She forced herself to unclench her fists and to smile lightly as she said in an unconcerned voice, "Maybe he will, maybe he won't. It doesn't really matter. What matters is that you're with me, Pete."

As she spoke to the tall blond boy beside her, she saw his face flush with pleasure. Then she saw that he was smiling at her as though she'd given him a wonderful present. Instead of feeling good about his obvious pleasure at her statement, Karen felt guilty. She liked Pete too much to hurt him or to use him in a game with Roger. Pete was a nice person and he deserved better than that. Even if she now knew it was Roger who truly attracted her, she could remember when one smile from Pete would have thrilled her. Karen's thoughts grew cloudier and cloudier. No. She wouldn't misuse Pete's love.

Then, in the next minute, she found herself smiling up at him with her most dazzling smile. Her voice sounded phony to her as she said in a deeper, softer tone than she usually used, "I mean it, Pete, I really appreciate all you've done for me." She reached out and put her hand lightly on his arm.

Pete stepped closer to her, bending his head down slightly as he whispered, "I love you, Karen. I'd do a lot more than this for you, you know."

She thought for a minute he was going to kiss her. Her mother must have thought the same thing because she called in a sharp voice, "Karen, will you come over here?"

Karen stepped back before Pete could put his arms around her. She smiled at him again and went to her mother, who was stacking flyers at both ends of the table. Her mother said in a loud voice, "Do you think it would be good to have them here?" Under her breath, she whispered, "What are you thinking of? Flirting with that boy on a public parking lot in broad daylight?"

Her mother sounded so old-fashioned and angry that Karen had to laugh as she protested, "I wasn't flirting, Mama. Just talking."

"Talking?" her mother said in a more normal tone. "Well, you'd have a hard time convincing anyone of that. You looked as though you were doing more than talking. In my day—"

"I'm sorry, Mama." Karen interrupted her to forestall a lecture about the good old days. It wasn't that her mother was so boring, it was just that she didn't feel like hearing any long speeches at the moment.

She just wanted to do a good job campaigning for queen and not think about anything else at all. When she thought, she hurt too much.

At least partly because she was trying to distract herself from thinking about her other troubles, Karen was more enthusiastic and friendly than she'd ever been. She thought the weather had something to do with her mood also. Last week had been as hot and humid as she could ever remember. She'd felt as though she were inside a dark and damp plastic bag. Today was an entirely different sort of day.

The sun was shining and the day was hot, but it was a pleasant summer heat. Karen loved the sunshine when there were blue skies and gentle breezes to go with it. Even on the parking lot pavement she was able to enjoy the perfect weather. Of course, it would have been nicer to be at the lake or down by the little stream where she'd run last Saturday. The sun seemed to bounce off the chrome and metal automobiles and shine at her with a fierce intensity. She had to concentrate in order to keep from squinting. But, for the most part, it was a good day to be outside talking to people.

She enjoyed the people more than she ever had. In all her attempts to campaign in the past, she'd found that she was very critical of people's comments or the way they looked—any little hint that they might vote for someone else made her feel awful. But today was different.

Around noon, she spent a long time talking to Mrs. Persip and her two sisters. The three old ladies didn't seem to be in any hurry to get out of the noonday sun and into the shopping mall, where they planned to have lunch. They seemed much more interested in talking with Karen, asking her all about her life. Karen was amused when Mrs. Persip asked such personal questions, especially since she was certain that the old lady knew most of the answers anyway.

Karen was surprised at how little her neighbor missed. She knew all about Lucy's dates. She asked, "You like that new boy? The dark one? Or is it the blond?"

Trying to be polite, Karen smiled and answered in a light voice, "Well, they're both nice. Which one do you think would be your choice?"

"Take the Peterson boy," Mrs. Persip advised. "You don't know anything at all about the new one's family."

Karen tried to laugh, though she was painfully aware that she would probably never have the choice to make. She stepped back from the three old ladies and said, "Enjoy your lunch, and be sure to vote for me."

Karen was amazed when they all three shook their heads to indicate that they would not vote for her. Mrs. Persip's sister explained, "We're related to the Melvilles. Charlotte's mother is married to my cousin's wife. So you see, we have to vote for the Melvilles."

"Of course," Karen agreed quickly. She watched the three old ladies walk away. Noting that they were exactly the same size and wore their hair cut in exactly the same way, she said to Lucy, "They look like triplets from behind."

Lucy snorted. "They're just alike," she said. "That's what I hate about small towns. Gossip, gossip, and everyone knows all of everyone's business."

Karen laughed and went over to talk to some other people who were walking by. By the time she came back Lucy was busy talking with a fellow she'd dated in high school. Karen didn't interrupt but stood aside and silently watched.

Her sister Lucy's auburn hair gleamed in the sun and threw off golden red sparks that seemed just as bright as the reflections from the metal cars. Lucy was a beautiful girl. Woman, Karen corrected herself. Lucy was a woman now, but she looked as young and beautiful as she had in high school. About the only difference was that Lucy kept her hair cut short and curly now instead of in the long, glamorous style she'd worn in high school. But her face and figure were as fresh and lovely as ever.

Now, as Karen watched her older sister talk with the man she'd been in love with ten years ago, she saw the way he had changed. His back seemed almost bent as he laughed and joked with Lucy. He was obviously enjoying himself and didn't seem very happy to see his wife and two small children when they walked up to join him. His wife looked very unhappy when she saw her husband chatting with Lucy.

Karen knew that his wife needn't worry. If there was anything that Lucy was definite about, it was married men. So often, since she'd started to work in the bank, she'd complained that the only men who paid any attention to her were married. Karen knew that her sister was feeling as though her choices in husbands were getting fewer and fewer. Even as she watched her beautiful sister charm her ex-boyfriend's wife, she knew that Lucy was unhappy. She had made a mistake not to go to college—Karen was certain of that.

But Karen knew she couldn't stand around worrying about Lucy all day long. She had work to do. She had things to accomplish. Once she decided she was going to win this contest, she knew that it was her job to put every bit of energy and enthusiasm that she could into the campaign. Today she had one of her very last chances to persuade people who might not vote at all to go to the trouble to fill out the newspaper application and write in the name of Karen Williams for Queen of the Harvest Parade.

She was very disappointed that Roger had deserted her and she was saddened that her friendship with Sue seemed to be, if not ending, at least fading away. Nevertheless, she did everything she could to keep a cheerful face as she talked to the people who were walking by her booth. Instead of hanging back and feeling shy, Karen was able to step out and give each person a hearty "Hello," offering her hand and asking them if they were planning to vote.

Many of the people seemed surprised that Karen was so friendly and many of them promised her that they would indeed vote for her. She wasn't sure that they were all telling the truth, but their friendly response to her campaigning made her feel good about herself.

The day seemed to pass in a whirl of activity and conversation. She talked with strangers and with people that she had known all her life. Off and on, she would think about Roger, and the thought was like a dark bird of sorrow flashing across the bright blue sky. But it was difficult to remain sad on such a lovely day and in the midst of so much excitement and enthusiasm about her chances in the contest. For quite a while now Karen had really wanted to win.

Around one o'clock Charlotte Melville drove up in a bright red convertible and set up a card table with some flyers of her own and two American flags at each end of the table. Karen knew that Charlotte's impromptu table did not have the same attraction and attention-getting ability as her own booth. Even so, Charlotte collected a crowd of admirers.

Karen walked across the parking lot to say hello to Charlotte and to wish her luck. Charlotte seemed surprised and she asked Karen, "Then you really aren't mad at me for doing the same thing you're doing?"

Karen laughed and said, "I told you, you're welcome to campaign. It's not my parking lot and it makes it more fun, doesn't it?"

Charlotte looked at Karen seriously for a moment and then shrugged her shoulders and said, "Not really, Karen. I don't think that having as sharp competition as you are is much fun at all. I'm afraid it's going to be a very close race."

Karen didn't know quite what to say to that, but she replied, "Well, close or not, I'm sure that you'll do very well in the contest. And I hope that we can be friends when it's all over."

Although Charlotte's face betrayed the doubt that she was feeling, the girl managed to smile and say quietly, "I hope so too, Karen. I really hope so. You're a nice person."

With that, Karen returned to her own booth and spent the rest of the afternoon with a peaceful feeling. She and Charlotte, though competitors, at least had a chance at friendship. Now that Roger and Sue had both deserted her, Karen was feeling very much as though she needed some new friends, and she had always thought Charlotte was a nice girl.

But not everyone had deserted her. Pete stayed with her all of the afternoon, running for Cokes and being generally attentive. As the afternoon wore on, she found that she had less and less to say to Pete. That discouraged her. In fact, she was forced to admit that, although she had once almost worshiped Pete, she was finding him dull. It made her sad but she was too honest with herself to deny her feelings.

While she was thinking about Pete, she was also missing Roger very much. Often she would lift her head and look out toward the edge of the parking lot to the deep green trees waving in the summer breeze. She would wonder where Roger was and exactly what he was doing. She wanted very much to question Pete or Lucy further about exactly what Roger had said when he had left, but she didn't want to betray how much it meant to her. If Roger had a date, she knew it was his right, and she had no business feeling as angry and upset as she was actually feeling. She searched her mind to try to discover what girl it would be that Roger would be dating. Who could he be interested in? Up until this last week, as far as she knew, Roger hadn't been interested in anyone else.

She smiled bitterly as she thought how quickly the tables had turned. Was it only a week ago that Roger had followed her down to the lake? Was it only two weeks ago that she had been so sure that Pete was the boy for her? She could hardly believe that the whole world had turned around as quickly and completely as it seemed to have done. She knew Roger would have been delighted to have a date with her before. Now she was almost crazy wondering where he was and what he was doing. Much as she tried to, she could not keep her mind from hoping that, somehow or other, they would be able to straighten things out between them. Yet she was sure things would never be all right again. She knew Roger was disappointed because she had decided to continue with the queen contest. Even so, she dreamed that she would have a chance to explain it all to him. She wanted that so much. She wanted that almost as much as she wanted to win the contest. She knew he would never believe that.

It was almost dark before Roger returned to the parking lot, carrying his guitar under his arm. He seemed to be totally relaxed about the fact that he had been gone all afternoon. Karen could not keep the snappishness from her voice as she asked, "Where were you?"

Roger looked surprised and answered quickly, "I told Pete that I had a date at the dentist's."

Relief washed through Karen's body as she realized that Roger had simply been in the dentist's chair and all of her worries had been for nothing. She said, "Oh, well, I didn't know if you were coming back or not."

Roger looked surprised again and shrugged his shoulders and said, "Well, here I am. Would you like me to play for the crowd now? How do you want to handle it, Karen?"

Karen tried to keep her voice businesslike as she replied, "You're doing this as a favor, Roger. I want you to do whatever you're comfortable with. As far as I'm concerned, anything at all you want to play will be fine with me."

His gray eyes twinkled as his lips tilted in a smile, and he asked, "It doesn't matter at all what I play?"

"No, no. Anything you want," Karen assured him. She was so grateful to discover that he had not been off with some other girl that she did not realize that he was teasing her.

"Okay, you asked for it," Roger said, and immediately launched into the first of many verses of "Old MacDonald's Farm." He sang "Old MacDonald's Farm" for over thirty minutes. During that period of time he collected a larger and larger audience. Karen had to admit that everyone seemed to enjoy the song very much. It was not long before the people who were standing around listening were joining in on the verses. Karen herself began to sing. She was able to relax and have a good time.

They sang their way through all of the barnyard animals and got into the animals that one would normally find in a zoo. After they completed the verses with zebras and lions and tigers, Roger went on to list all of the exotic animals that he could think of, including iguanas and aardvarks. When he got to aardvarks there was a moment's silence, since no one in the audience could even begin to imagine what sort of a sound an aardvark would make. Finally, Roger made a kind of buzzing sound and it trailed off into the night. He dropped his guitar and bowed. The people who were gathered around him clapped enthusiastically.

When the applause had died down, Roger said to the group, "And now I'd like to introduce the next Queen of Wilks County, Miss Karen Williams. Let's have a big hand for Karen, folks."

The audience, which consisted mostly of small children and their parents, clapped enthusiastically for Karen as she took a bow. They did seem to have enjoyed Roger's song and Karen knew that it would help her campaign.

As the audience drifted off, Karen turned to Roger

and said as warmly as she could, "Roger, I want to thank you. I know that you don't really approve of this Harvest Queen contest and I know that you don't really approve of my campaigning to be the queen, but it's really very sweet of you to help me out."

Roger shrugged his shoulders again and said, "But I promised I would help you, Karen."

A sharp stab of disappointment surged through Karen's body as she realized that Roger was helping her, not because he cared about her, but because he cared about keeping his promise. Her worst fear was true, then; Roger really was not interested in her at all. This bitter knowledge was confirmed when, two hours later, he said, "I hope you'll understand when I make my excuses and leave. I promised my mom and dad that I would attend a party they're having tonight. The dinner's at seven o'clock and I have to get back. I'm sorry. I would like to have helped more, Karen. Honestly, I would."

Karen extended her hand and smiled at him. She was trying to make her smile pleasant and to mask the pain she was feeling at Roger's second desertion of the day. She said, in as formal a voice as she could manage, "Thank you again, Roger. I really do appreciate the help you've given us."

"Us?" Roger asked.

Karen flushed and stammered, "By us I mean my mother and Lucy and me."

Roger shook his head and said in a lightly critical voice, "You still aren't in this campaign for yourself, are you, Karen? You're still doing it to please other people."

Karen opened her mouth to try to explain to Roger

exactly why she had decided to stay in the campaign despite her own personal reluctance and then, as Roger looked at his watch with an anxious eye, she closed her mouth and shook her head. It wouldn't do any good to try and explain things. All she said was, "Well, thanks anyway. I know that you went out of your way to help me." And with that she turned and walked over to Pete. She put her hand on Pete's shoulder, smiled up at Pete, and asked, "What time do you think we should close? About nine thirty?"

Pete looked down at her and said, "I think we should close whenever you want, Karen. Are you tired?"

Karen smiled sweetly at Pete and shook her head. She laughed lightly, hoping that her voice conveyed the affection and slightly flirtatious air that she was striving for. Then she answered, "Not too tired to go dancing afterward, if that's okay with you?"

Roger was standing, holding his guitar at his side, looking as though he felt slightly awkward. Karen was upset enough herself to be glad that he was also feeling pain. She pretended not to notice as Roger turned and walked into the deepening dusk.

The minute Roger was gone from sight Karen dropped her hand from Pete's shoulder, dropped the smile from her lips, and let her shoulders sag with sadness.

Pete asked anxiously, "You're tired, aren't you, Karen?"

"A little," she admitted.

"Then maybe we'd better not go out this evening," Pete said. "We have a lifetime to go dancing, don't we?"

There was a question in Pete's voice that Karen felt demanded a commitment, but Karen was in no condition to give him any sort of serious answer at all. She shrugged her shoulders, blinked her eyes to keep the tears from them, tried her very hardest to smile at Pete, and asked, "Do we? I suppose we do, Pete. I suppose so."

14

During the last week of the contest, Karen campaigned as hard as any of the contestants. Like Charlotte Melville and the other girls, Karen began to make door-to-door house calls. Though she found them initially painful, she began to feel better about them when she discovered that most of the people who answered the door were very courteous. Several of them invited her in to sit and chat. Often people would offer her cookies or coffee, and many of them seemed to be quite interested in her campaign. Not once, but several times, she got into conversations with older people who were interested in teenagers. They talked about what the youth of today thought about modern life.

On more than one occasion, Karen found herself explaining in great detail exactly why she had chosen to become a Harvest Queen contestant. One or two people seemed to disapprove of the contest in general. Others didn't think teenage girls should campaign so actively for the role. But most of the people accepted the contest as a wonderful part of living in a small town.

Karen was pleasantly surprised to discover how many of the people she visited had already decided to vote for her. As the week progressed, she began to be more and more hopeful that she might win. Lucy, her mother, Pete, and everyone else she talked to seemed to agree that her greatest competition would come from Charlotte Melville. Charlotte had a very large family of cousins and aunts and uncles living all over the county.

Since the Melvilles were so numerous and since so many of them lived in outlying areas, Karen really had no way of assessing her chances. Lucy and her mother insisted that no one would consider voting for anyone else.

Pete was just as prejudiced as her mother and sister. He talked constantly about when Karen was queen and what they would do before the parade and what they would do after the festivities.

Pete would be one of the six young escorts for the queen and he talked as though there was no question that it would be Karen he'd be escorting.

Karen was deeply grateful for the loyalty and the confidence that Pete and her family exhibited on her behalf, though she was not as optimistic as they were. She felt that she had a good chance, but she did not feel that she had an absolute guarantee of victory.

She knew that she had put herself behind by not being as enthusiastic as she should have been at the beginning of the campaign. Now it was up to her to make it up by working just as hard as she possibly could. She was determined to do her very best.

Up until the actual day of the voting, Karen tried to convince her mother and Lucy that they should be prepared for the worst. But there was really no way that she could convince them that there was even a chance that she might lose.

On the day of the voting, Karen decided to stay home rather than continue going door to door. Lucy and her mother weren't so sure that that was a good idea. As a matter of fact, they suggested that she might consider following Sue's original campaign plan of doing last-minute telephoning all over the county. When they had first planned the campaign, Sue had insisted that a chain of telephone calls on the last day of the campaign would get Karen votes. She thought it would work better than any other thing that they could possibly have done. Karen had been against the idea, partly because she didn't want to be a pest but mostly because she didn't want to waste the money. It hurt her to see her family's resources dwindle so rapidly, and a large telephone bill would make things worse.

That morning Sue called and asked her if she wanted help with the telephoning. Karen said as pleasantly and as firmly as she could, "We're not going to be telephoning today, Sue. I've decided against it."

Sue, who had not been around very much lately but who obviously still considered herself a director of Karen's campaign, insisted that was a mistake. "You'll be sorry," Sue warned. "You'll pick up a lot of votes if you call them today."

Karen shook her head even though she was talking on the telephone and said, "I don't think so, Sue. I think if we interrupt people during the day, we may lose votes rather than gain them. I've given it some serious thought and that's what I believe."

"Well, what does Lucy think?" Sue asked.

Karen smiled into the receiver as she remembered the conversation she'd had with Lucy and her mother last night. She assured Sue that both her mother and sister were willing to let Karen make that decision for herself. She did not go on to tell Sue how very supportive they had been. Sue might take it as criticism of her own recent loss of interest in Karen's campaign.

Karen said, "So I thank you for your offer to help, Sue, but the truth of the matter is, the campaign is over."

There was a pause and then Sue said, "I'm warning you, Karen—if you don't campaign today, you're going to lose votes. Charlotte Melville has got every one of her cousins out going door to door. I know because she told me so."

Karen wondered why Sue had been talking to Charlotte. Was Sue helping Charlotte? Karen quickly dismissed that idea. Sue, though angry at her, could never be disloyal enough to switch to Charlotte Melville. Sue had never been able to stand Charlotte and nothing would have happened to change that opinion.

Karen tried to remain as calm and reasonable as she could as she said to Sue, "I've done the best I can, and if Charlotte wins, she wins. There is nothing more that I'm going to do today. I'm sure that anything I did today would simply annoy people. People have made up their minds and I'll have to take my chances."

Instead of arguing, Sue said, "Good luck," and hung up the phone.

Karen was dismayed that she had won the argument so quickly. She knew that Sue's fast capitulation was more an indication of Sue's remaining anger than agreement. Sadness washed over Karen as she thought how this campaign had driven her and Sue apart. It had been a long friendship and Karen hated the feeling that it was cooling. Nevertheless, Karen knew that she would never bow to Sue's wishes again when she thought Sue was wrong. From now on she was determined to be her own person.

She thought back to the conversation that she'd had with her mother and Lucy last night and she felt very, very good. They had discussed the telephone campaign and had listened carefully to what Karen had to say. After Karen had explained her reasons for not wanting to have the telephone campaign, she had waited to hear Lucy and her mother's objections. She had been expecting that she would have to fight for her right to stick to her own opinions. Instead Lucy and her mother surprised her by saying whatever she did would be right. They said that so far everything she had done was very effective and that her judgment was perfectly good and sound.

Karen had looked from one to the other in amazement and had said simply and quietly, "Thank you. Thank you for your confidence in me."

As she thought of that wonderful discussion, a great warmth and joy ran through her. She knew that the campaign, whether she won or lost, had been good for her. She had learned a lot about handling people. At least, she had learned a lot about handling *some* people.

Unfortunately, she had not been able to handle the one person that she cared the most about in the world. Roger had not been around at all this week. Roger, she was now sure, was out of her life forever. Several times she had gone to the telephone to dial his number, but each time her courage had failed her. She was resigned to the fact that whatever might have been between Roger and her would never be. Yet, though she was resigned to the loss of Roger, she was not resigned to the loss of the feelings that Roger had stirred in her. She remembered the shared kisses. She could not keep from reliving the feelings that those kisses had stirred up in her or dwelling on those few magic moments they had shared by the lake. Roger might be gone forever, but she was convinced that she would never settle for anything less.

If Roger was gone, somehow, somewhere she would find another boy that she could feel that way about. And though she regretted it, she was honest enough with herself to know that Pete would never be that boy. He was a sweet boy, but he was not the boy for her.

As Karen had worked her way through the last week of the campaign, she had resolved she must somehow find the strength to explain to Pete exactly what she was feeling. It would be painful, but she would find the words to do that. She owed him her honesty.

Karen dreaded the idea of talking to Pete seriously and she told herself that she would not even try until after the results of the Harvest Queen contest were in. If she won, she would wait until after the parade. She owed Pete a lot for his help with the contest and she felt that, in a way, she had been unfair to him. She knew she was judging him by standards that he would not even understand.

As the day of the voting wore on, Karen spent more and more of her time worrying about exactly what she was going to say to Pete and how she was going to say it. But she was clear in her determination that she would talk to him. She was never going to deceive Pete again. He was too good for that. He deserved better treatment. As she thought of Pete, her heart ached for the loss of Roger. Not that Roger had ever really *been* her boyfriend, but those kisses must have meant that he was interested in her.

She wasn't as nervous about the voting as she might have been. For one thing, she thought she probably would win. She knew if she did not win, she would at least have the pleasure of knowing that she had tried her very best. Deep in her heart she also held the slight hope that if she should lose the contest she might win Roger. She was quite sure that Roger not only disapproved of the contest, but would disapprove of any girl who was Harvest Queen for Wilks County.

These thoughts whirled around in her head as she tried to spend the day relaxing, looking at magazines, doing her nails, washing her hair, and cleaning out the refrigerator. By four o'clock in the afternoon, everything in the apartment was so tidy that she could find nothing else to do except scrub the kitchen and bathroom floors.

She knew that it would be at least six o'clock before she would hear the results of the contest. Ballots for the contest had appeared in yesterday's newspapers and paperboys and papergirls were to make the rounds of every house on their routes before noon. Then they would deliver the ballots to the newspaper before three o'clock in the afternoon. They would count the ballots at the newspaper as quickly as possible. Since there would be over three thousand ballots, the newspaper editor had warned all the contestants that it would be at least six o'clock in the evening before the results were in.

Even so, Karen jumped every time the telephone rang that afternoon. The first call was from Lucy, who wanted to know if she had heard anything. The second call was from Sue, who wanted to know the same thing. The third and fourth calls were from her mother and the fifth call was Lucy again. When her mother called another time at five thirty, Karen could not keep the snappishness out of her voice. She said, "Mama, if the phone is busy, I'll never hear. Don't call me—I'll call you."

Almost the minute she hung up the phone, it rang another time. Certain that it would be either Sue or Pete, she lifted the receiver from the hook and said, "Hello," with annoyance in her voice.

It was the editor of the Wilks County *Gazette*, John Murphy. Mr. Murphy said, "Karen, I have the final results in front of me and I have some news for you and I want you to know . . ."

Karen's heart began racing. Her ears began ringing and her pulse flashed so rapidly that she wasn't sure she would be able to hear what he was saying if Mr. Murphy finally got around to telling her whether she had won or lost. But when his voice came through on the other end and she heard the words ". . . so you will be Queen . . ." Karen was able to register the fact that she had won.

"Thank you," she said. "Thank you for calling me so quickly. Thank you, thank you so much." All she could really think to say was "Thank you," but she felt that that was, under the circumstances, exactly the best thing to say.

She called her mother at the bakery. As soon as she announced the news to her mother, she could hear her mother shouting the news to all of the customers in the bakery and she could hear a smattering of applause at the good news. Karen was so delighted for her mother that it was almost as though it were her mother's victory—not her own.

By the time she finished talking to her mother, Lucy's bank was closed, so there was no way to call her.

She would have to wait until Lucy came in the front door to give her the news. Karen called Pete on the telephone and told him that she had won the contest.

"I'm not surprised," Pete answered in a matter of fact voice, "but I guess you wanted me to know officially. Now I can order the flowers to wear on your dress. What color?"

Karen thought about the two dresses she'd tried in the best dress shop in town. She realized she must call Mrs. Wilson as quickly as possible and let her know which of the dresses she would be wearing for the parade. She thought sadly for a moment about the simple yellow cotton dress she would have chosen for herself. But she knew that it would be the fancier pink dress after all.

"I'll wear the pink dress, Pete," Karen said.

"Then white flowers?" Pete asked.

"Oh, Pete, please don't buy me flowers," Karen said. "Please let me buy my own flowers."

She knew that her reaction to his proffered gift would hurt him, and the minute she had said those words she wanted to take them back. After all, she had promised herself she would say nothing to Pete until after the parade. Why was she balking at a simple little thing like a corsage? Pete had talked about buying her flowers for the last three weeks, teasing her that he would bring her yellow daisies to wear on the pink dress and other flower color combinations that would be just as bad.

Pete said with a grave tone of voice, "If you don't want white flowers, Karen, all you have to do is tell me what to buy. But I will be the one to bring you this corsage. It's something we've planned."

"Of course it is," Karen said with a warm rush of concern and guilt. "But I think I would like a deep red flower—roses maybe. Maybe deep red roses to show off the pink dress." She hoped that her voice sounded normal and that Pete wouldn't pick up the sadness that lay behind the pleasure of victory. As she talked to Pete, she was wishing that he were Roger. She felt very sad about that.

They talked until Lucy came in the front door, calling out in a loud voice, "I heard you won!"

Karen said goodby to Pete and hung up the phone. She turned to run and hug her older sister. They threw their arms around each other, hugging each other tight, and danced around the small apartment living room. Then Lucy drew back, holding her hands on Karen's shoulders, and looked at her younger sister with bright, gleaming happiness in her eyes. Her voice seemed vibrant with joy as she asked, "Now tell me, Karen, aren't you happy that you're going to be queen?"

Karen thought that beneath the light teasing and happy tone there was a serious question and so she answered seriously, "Yes, Lucy, I'm happy I'm going to be queen. As long as I was in the contest I'm happy I won. I'm happy that you're happy. I'm happy that mother is happy. I'm happy that I'm going to be queen."

"But for yourself?" Lucy asked.

Karen thought that over carefully. Wasn't that what Roger had asked her the other day? Wasn't she in this contest for herself? She thought a long time and finally answered, "Lucy, it's complicated. I'm not sure I would ever have entered the race for queen if it weren't for the fact that you and mother were queens before me. But then since you and mother were *you*, you had to be queens of the parade. Since I couldn't be anyone but *myself*, and being myself means being your little sister and Mama's little daughter, then . . ."

Lucy laughed and interrupted, "The way you make your explanations are so complicated, Karen. I asked you a simple question. Are you happy for yourself or are you happy just for us?"

Karen tried one more time to answer, "I'm happy for myself because I've learned a lot during this campaign. I've learned what's important to me and I've learned what's not important to me. I've learned to stand up for what I believe in. I've learned to talk to people. Yes, I'm glad to be Harvest Queen and I'm happy that I'll be following in the tradition—in the footsteps . . ."

Here Lucy interrupted one more time, holding her hands skyward in protest and saying in a laughter-filled voice, "Enough. Enough. You sound like you're making one more contest campaign speech, but the campaign is over, Karen. And *I'm* happy you've won."

The telephone rang and Lucy said, "You might as well answer it. All the calls will be for you tonight. Your big day begins right this very minute."

Karen went over to the telephone and answered it.

Without identifying herself, Sue said, "Charlotte Melville's demanding a recount. Did you ever hear anything so awful in your whole life?"

"Wait a minute," Karen said. "How do you know Charlotte Melville wants a recount?"

"Well, I just know," Sue said. "I . . . I . . ."

Karen asked, "Did you call Charlotte?"

"No, no, no. Charlotte called me," Sue answered quickly. "When they called her to say that she had lost, they told her that she lost only by forty-three votes. She and her mother have decided that they want a recount. They're going down to the *Gazette* office right now. You've got to call the editor at the *Gazette* and tell him that you protest. You've got a right to protest."

"Wait a minute," Karen said. "If Charlotte thinks

that there's been a mistake, then she has every right to demand a recount. I'm not going to protest, Sue."

"But you have to," Sue said.

Karen said quietly, "No Sue, I don't *have* to. But you haven't congratulated me. Congratulate me and hang up. I'm going to call Charlotte right away."

"Are you going to tell Charlotte that she can't have a recount?" Sue demanded.

"Of course not," Karen said. "I guess you can congratulate me later." With that, Karen hung up the telephone and immediately picked it up again and dialed Charlotte's number.

Charlotte's mother answered the phone and Karen identified herself and asked to speak with Charlotte. Her mother said quickly, "Charlotte doesn't want to talk to you."

Karen said as politely as she could, "Mrs. Melville, would you ask Charlotte if she wants to talk to me? She might and, if not, I can talk with you about what I have to say."

There was a long silence on the other end of the phone and then Charlotte came to the telephone and said in a tear-soaked voice, "Hi, Karen."

Karen took a deep breath and said quickly, "Charlotte, if you want a recount, you have every right to demand one. If the editor at the *Gazette* doesn't want to give you a recount, then you tell him to call me. Better yet, would you like me to go down to the office with you? We can both demand a recount. Because if you're the winner, then you'll be a fine queen."

There was a long pause at the other end of the phone and then Charlotte said in a deep but determined voice, "Karen, I don't know how you heard that I was thinking about asking for a recount, but I'm not. There was some talk of it over here. I wasn't part of the talk and I don't want a recount. You won the contest fair and square. It's all over. That's all there is to it. Congratulations."

Then Karen knew. The recount had not been Charlotte's idea at all. It had been Sue's idea. She must have been helping Charlotte with her campaign.

Karen said, "It was Sue's idea, wasn't it?"

Charlotte answered quickly, "I don't want to talk about it, Karen. All I want to do is say that, for sure, I'm not going to ask for a recount. Congratulations and have a good day. I'll see you in school in a week or so, okay?" With that, Charlotte hung up the telephone.

Karen turned and said to her sister, "Sue's been helping Charlotte. Sue wanted Charlotte to demand a recount. Sue's really not my friend at all."

Lucy looked at Karen's stricken face and said, "Oh, Karen, I'm so sorry," and ran and hugged her sister again, this time to comfort rather than to celebrate.

It was only a short time before Karen was able to recover her sense of elation at having won the contest. When her mother came in from work, she was able to celebrate their victory without any trace of sorrow. By now Karen had figured out that no matter how much sadness there was in the world, there was always a way to find joy. She was also learning that there was no joy without at least a tinge of sadness.

"This is my victory," Karen whispered to herself. "I am going to enjoy it for all it's worth."

15

The day of the Harvest Parade began early with a bright yellow sun rising in the east and spreading a rosy light over Wilks County. The rosy light mixed with the darkness to produce a magical robin's-egg sky so that by the time Karen rolled out of bed at seven thirty in the morning she knew it was going to be a wonderful day.

She pulled on her bright yellow seersucker robe and went into the kitchen to make breakfast for herself and her mother and sister. Within ten minutes the coffee was bubbling in the pot. The smell of the Colombian roast brought Lucy and her mother out of their beds and into the kitchen to watch as Karen tended the sizzling bacon in the flat black skillet.

Her mother's first words to her were, "Be careful. Don't burn yourself. You don't want your hands all spotted on this day."

Karen laughed and teased her mother. "I'll be glad when I'm finished being a queen and can go back to being a normal, ordinary teenager. It seems as if you worry more about my appearance than anything else. Why aren't you worrying about the burns hurting me, Mama?"

Her mother refused to rise to the bait. Instead she went to the refrigerator and pulled some frozen Danish sweet cakes out of the freezer compartment. She said, "I thought we could use these this morning. This ought to be a good hearty breakfast because it will be a long time before we eat again."

Karen said, "Oh, they look good. That's wonderful."

The three women worked together to complete the breakfast. As they were sitting down at the kitchen table to begin eating the Danish coffee rolls and the bacon and eggs, Lucy said, "I have news. I guess this is as good a time as any to tell it. I've been making some decisions of my own."

Karen looked up from buttering a coffee roll and said in a teasing voice, "Decisions, Lucy? Are you getting married?" She knew that nothing made her sister angrier than to be teased about her single status.

Lucy didn't respond to Karen's joke. Instead she said, "I've been thinking about this for a long time and I have decided that I'm finally going to go through with it. This is a good day to tell you because this is a kind of special day—a day of endings and beginnings."

Karen wondered what it could be that made her sister sound so eloquent. Usually Lucy was very plain-spoken. But this morning she seemed more serious than usual.

Lucy continued, "I have decided that the time has come in my life for me to figure out exactly how I want to spend the rest of my life. It seems that some of us take a little longer to find out what we want than others. But I think I have really figured out what I want to do. I am going to go back to school."

There was silence around the table. Neither Karen nor her mother said anything, so Lucy continued, "You see, I should have gone to college when I graduated from high school. At that time I just didn't seem to get it together enough. I thought that I would go the next year and the next year. Then I thought that I was too old. Now I'm twenty-five and, if I don't go soon, I'll never get there. So I'm going in the fall. I am going to take my share of Aunt Alice's money and the money that I've saved from my job. I think I'll be able to get a part-time job. I may not be able to finish in four years, but I think I can finish eventually. So what if I'm twenty-nine or thirty years old when I graduate from college? I'm going to be twenty-nine or thirty years old whether I graduate from college or not."

Lucy stopped talking and looked at her mother and then her sister. She was obviously waiting for some kind of reaction. The only reaction she got for quite a while was silence. Karen, for her part, was thinking how much braver and much more mature Lucy was than she had ever really given her credit for. Their mother didn't seem to know what to think.

Finally, Marsha Williams said, "I'll miss you. I never really thought much about you going to college, Lucy. I guess I always thought that you would stay right here in Wilks. But, of course you should go to college. You're a smart girl. You should have your chance. You can take my share of Aunt Alice's money too. With that you should be able to make it."

Then Marsha Williams seemed to reconsider. "No,

you can only take half my share. The other half will have to go for Karen's education."

Karen turned to her mother and said, "You're a good mother and I know you mean it, but I'm not going to take your money for college. You've already done too much for me."

Lucy chimed in, "Keep your money, Mama. I'll take the money Aunt Alice left me and Karen will take the money Aunt Alice left her. You need money, too. It's time you started thinking about living a little bit for yourself."

Marsha Williams looked as though she were going to cry. She picked up the Danish and buttered it and then pulled it into little pieces. When the silence around the kitchen table got so heavy that she was really uncomfortable, she said, "Well, yes. Yes. You're right, of course. It is time I started living for myself." Then she looked at Karen and said simply, "Karen, I know you never wanted to be in this contest. But I'm glad you won. If that's wrong of me, I'm sorry, but I'm glad you won. But you're right, Lucy—I will start living for myself." And then her mouth turned up into a smile and her blue eyes began to twinkle and she said, "Tomorrow. I promise you tomorrow I'll start. But today I'll live for Karen. This is Karen's day."

The more Karen thought about it, the happier she was that Lucy had decided to go back to college. She had been worried about her sister. She thought Lucy's life was really at a dead end in this small country town. When her sister went to college many things would open up for her.

As for herself, Karen knew that she would have to begin making plans of her own very soon. There would be one more year of high school and then she would have to go on her way as well. But Karen was determined that she wouldn't think of things like that today. Planning for a future, while not as sad as losing a friendship, still came under the category of serious subjects. Now that she was Queen of the Harvest Parade, Karen was determined that she was going to enjoy that victory to its fullest. There would be no serious subjects today. There would be no thinking of tall, slim young men with dark brown eyes who made her knees tremble and her heart melt. No, she would not think of Roger. She would not think of Sue. She would not think of anything at all except the wonderful experience that was before her.

At nine o'clock she went into the bedroom and took down the frilly pink dress that she would be wearing as queen. The dress was in a soft fabric, but the skirt stood out with full petticoats. Even though the fabric was soft and filmy and felt wonderful to her touch, the skirt seemed to move as though it had a life of its own. Karen slipped the dress over her head and had her sister help her zip up. She stepped in front of her full-length mirror to examine her appearance.

Karen took a deep breath and breathed out, "Oh, I do look like a princess!" And indeed she did. The full skirt pointed out her slim waist. Her arms looked golden brown and beautiful in comparison to the bright pink of the dress. Her auburn hair seemed to sparkle with red and gold highlights.

As she applied her makeup, she was not surprised to discover that her fingers were trembling with excitement. Her eyes were shining more brightly than usual. The day had begun and it was going to be wonderful for her. She was enjoying getting dressed in the beginning of her day and she intended to enjoy everything else—all the way until the end of the dance that evening.

At exactly ten forty-five Pete knocked at the door. He was carrying a corsage of deep red roses with a small spray of bridal wreath tucked between the lovely red flowers. He handed the corsage to Karen and advanced to kiss her lightly on the cheek, saying, "You look beautiful, Karen."

Karen linked her arm in Pete's and looked up at him and smiled and said, "Thank you, Pete. I'm glad you're here." It was the truth. She was glad to be walking out the front door of her apartment on the arm of Pete Peterson, the boy that she had known since kindergarten.

She rode to the beginning of the parade grounds with Pete. Lucy and her mother followed in their car. It was difficult squeezing the large pink gown into Pete's little yellow Volkswagen, but it added to the fun and excitement. On the drive to the parade she and Pete talked of the contest and other people. The conversation was light, pleasant, and easy.

Karen was glad that Pete wasn't carrying on about his romantic interest in her. She didn't want to feel a hypocrite. She had definitely decided that she was going to tell Pete when the parade was over that she was not interested in him. She did not want to be put in the position of being a phony in the meantime. She was grateful to Pete for keeping the conversation as light as it was.

They pulled into the street that would lead them out to the park where the parade would begin. They drove down a narrow road with many trees on each side of the road. They were all alone and Karen felt for a moment as though she were indeed a queen entering into a magical kingdom.

To her surprise, Pete pulled off from the road into a small clearing and parked the car. Karen felt her heart sink. She was sure that Pete was going to insist on kissing her before the parade began and she was prepared to put him off by telling him that it would smear her makeup. But to her surprise, Pete lifted Karen's hand from her lap and held her hand in his two larger hands and said softly, "Karen, there's something I want to talk to you about."

Karen was terrified that Pete was going to ask her to get engaged or ask for a greater commitment from her in some other way. Her answer would have to be no, and that would be a tragic beginning to this day of victory. Karen said nothing, letting her hand lie quietly between Pete's hands. She ignored the light caressing fingers that pressed against her own and listened as Pete said, "I just want to tell you, I'm glad that we're doing this together, Karen. I want you to know it means a lot to me."

"It means a lot to me, too, Pete," Karen said.

Pete shook his head and looked sad for a moment. Then he said, "Yes. But it means different things to both of us. I'm crazy about you, Karen. I've been crazy about you ever since we started dating, and I know you're not crazy about me."

"Oh, Pete," Karen said. There was nothing more to add to that sad exclamation.

"It's all right, Karen," Pete reassured her gently. "I've known it for a couple of weeks now. I guess I'm just not sophisticated enough for you."

"It isn't that, Pete," Karen said. "It's . . ."

Pete lifted a finger and pressed it against her lips,

shutting the words in so that she could not continue. Then he said, "It's not anything we need to talk about, Karen. A guy can tell when feelings change. Your feelings have changed for me and I know it. I guess I just wanted to let you know that it's all right. That's all. We don't have to talk about it any more today if you don't want to."

He lifted his fingers from her lips and bent to kiss her lightly. Then he whispered, "Goodbye, Karen. It was fun."

Karen was surprised that Pete was sensitive enough to understand her feelings so quickly. She would like to have explained to him, but she really felt that explanations would be more hurtful than silence. Instead she simply said, "You've been a good friend, Pete, and I hope you always will be."

He nodded quietly, turned on the ignition, pulled out of the parking space off the side of the road, pulled back onto the road, and drove her on into the parking lot of the park. After he parked the car, Pete ran around to open the car door for her. Karen gathered her full pink skirt into her hands. She stepped out of the little yellow Volkswagen onto the dark parking lot. Then she stepped quickly onto the grass, holding her long formal skirt high over her ankles so that she did not trail it into the dirt and get it dusty. As she began walking toward the site where the floats were waiting, the president of the Chamber of Commerce came running toward her, looking excited and out of breath. Behind him was the newspaper photographer from the *Gazette*.

The president of the Chamber of Commerce said, "Hurry up, Karen. Hurry up. It's time for your float to leave."

Karen gasped and said, "I'm sorry," and ran across

the grassy lawn to the float that was parked and waiting beside the street.

Despite the warnings of the Chamber of Commerce president, her float was not ready to go. There were three men still working on it. The float was on the base of a flatbed truck and there was a large platform fastened onto the truck. Two men were underneath the truck making final adjustments so that the float would ride securely in the parade.

Karen could see that the high school band was ready to go. They were lined up carefully. She saw her high school music teacher standing in front of the band, looking hot and sweaty and overweight in her red velvet hat and red jacket with gold buttons. She saw several kids she knew from school. Most of them waved to her and she waved back, feeling very happy and proud to be queen of the parade.

By the time the parade got started, it was thirty minutes late, which was not surprising. Pete grinned at her and said, "Right on schedule—for Wilks County, that is."

Karen didn't mind that the parade was late. She didn't mind standing around on one foot waiting for the men who were putting her float together. When the other escorts came over to join her and Pete, she enjoyed being the center of attention. All six young men were friends of hers—boys she knew from high school. They all looked handsome and very different in their white dinner jackets and bow ties. As Karen stood in the center of their circle, talking to them, she was thinking how much difference clothing could make. Suddenly she thought of Roger and the white shirts he always wore. Thinking of Roger was like feeling a sharp pain run through her body. Why, on this perfect day, couldn't life be perfect?

If Karen's thoughts made her silent, her escorts didn't seem to mind. She wasn't surprised when they moved into a conversation about the baseball season that was just over and the football season that was soon to begin. Even though she was queen of the parade, she knew that for these boys with whom she had gone to school since kindergarten she was not exactly a glamorous celebrity.

When the parade actually got started, Karen felt the excitement that had been growing in her deepen. She felt for the first time all morning as though this parade were something that would be a very special experience for her. When she watched the high school band march off to lead the parade, she stood beside the band and waved goodbye to them as though she were indeed a queen saying goodbye to her troops.

It was with great pleasure that she then turned and walked back to her own float and let Pete help her climb onto the platform and prepare for the ride.

Her float was one of the largest ones in the parade. It would be last. The flat platform was painted a bright blue. The edges of that platform were decorated with crepe paper flowers.

There was a canopy of lavender nylon marquisette draped over half of the platform. Under the lavender canopy sat a large chair painted with gold paint. Karen was given a gold crown to wear and she was surprised that it was as lightweight as it was. "Plastic," the man from the Lions Club explained. "In the old days the crown was made from metal, but it was too heavy. You're luckier than your mother. She had to wear the old-fashioned one."

There were tall tin cans covered with gold foil at each edge of the platform. The cans were filled with gladiolus and other summer flowers. Karen knew that the float would probably look corny to some people, but she thought it was very pretty. She said quite honestly, "I think everything is just beautiful."

The Lions Club members looked pleased and hopped off the float, leaving it to Karen and her six escorts to take their places. The photographer from the paper took several photos and then the float pulled out onto the street. Karen felt the rumbling of the truck under her feet and it seemed as if the vibration from the truck filled her with feelings of joy and enthusiasm.

The parade route started at the park and wound down the outskirts of the town of Wilks onto the highway. It went as far as the shopping center on the edge of town and then back through some of the neighborhood streets to the main street of town. It would end by passing the main street, where most of the people would be watching, finally finishing at the high school gym field. Karen knew the float would pass right by Roger's door and she wondered if he would be there, watching her triumphal journey. Or would he think it was too corny?

You're not going to worry about that, Karen reminded herself. She forced herself to smile and wave at the first cluster of people they passed as they pulled out of the park grounds and onto the streets. Soon she was honestly enjoying the parade again. She felt as good as she'd hoped to feel, and if thoughts of Roger poked through her determined cheerfulness, she pushed them away.

It was a lot like watching your life go by, Karen thought as the parade float rumbled by Mrs. Murphy's door, past her first grade school, past the apple tree where she'd fallen and broken her ankle when she was nine. She smiled and waved at the people who were waving to her. Whenever she saw someone she knew, she greeted them by name. It seemed to her that she knew most of the people they passed on the parade route.

As they drew closer to Roger's house, Karen felt her cheerful happiness tense into a forced determination not to be disappointed, even if Roger weren't there. But even so, she was leaning forward, searching for Roger, long before they got to his block.

She was so busy looking for him down the block that it was startling when he appeared right under her nose. He called out, "Hello, Queen Karen—here's something for you."

Roger lifted a bouquet of garden flowers up to her as he ran along beside the float. Karen looked at his handsome, smiling face. His gray eyes seemed to dance in the sun and his dark brown hair looked so shiny and thick that she wanted to reach over and touch the heavy curls. She bent over and took the flowers, saying, "Thank you, Roger. I thought you might not be here."

"Not be here? Miss the greatest cultural event in Wilks County? You must be kidding."

When he saw Karen's face slip into a disappointed shyness, he must have sensed that she didn't know whether or not he was teasing. He said in a softer voice, "You look like a queen, Karen. Are you having fun?"

Roger was trotting along beside the float, but Karen knew they would soon turn the corner and be on the highway. When they got there, he wouldn't be able to keep up, even if he wanted to. The knowledge that their conversation would be short gave her courage. She asked, "Will you come to the dinner and dance?"

"I don't think so," Roger said. He looked over at Pete, who was standing with the other five boys, carefully staring up at the blue sky.

"I need to talk to you," Karen said. "Meet me at the bandstand at six thirty. Please?"

Before she could get an answer from Roger, the float began to turn the corner. She yelled back at him. "Promise you'll try?"

"I promise," Roger said, and he stopped chasing the parade. Karen watched his tall, slim form grow smaller as her float jounced along the highway.

The next few minutes of the parade seemed like a dream to Karen, she was so busy thinking about Roger and her conversation with him. She'd done it again, hadn't she? One more time she'd pushed herself forward, demanding his attention. Would he really come to the bandstand at six thirty? And if he did, would she be able to find the words to explain things to him?

But even as she worried about these things, she was waving her hand to the people on the sidewalks, calling out to them and bowing from the waist. She was Karen the Queen for this one day and she didn't want to let anyone down. She was determined that she would behave the way a real queen would behave. She would not let her personal hopes and problems get into the way of performing her duties.

By this time they were almost an hour late. Karen was afraid that many of the country people who had come to see the parade would be so hot and bored that they would go home. Though the idea didn't really bother her for herself, she worried that her mother and Lucy would be disappointed if the streets weren't jammed to watch her victorious entry into town. But despite the lateness of the hour and the broiling overhead sun, there were plenty of people on the main street. Karen was delighted to see that many of them were farmers from the outlying areas. The men were wearing brand-new coveralls and the women were wearing their best pants suits or dresses. Some of the women were wearing wide straw hats. A few of the hats had flowers or ribbons tied to them.

The parade itself was a simple one. It contained the high school band and about twelve floats built by various organizations in the town. The Chamber of Commerce float was one of the fanciest ones because it had lots of corn stalks on it and a couple of funny-looking scarecrows. The best thing about the Chamber of Commerce float was the mayor, dressed in a scarecrow costume. He was busy tossing out small bags of candy corn to children on the main street.

Karen's float had been built by her sponsor, the Lions Club. Other floats were built by organizations like the Elks and the Women's Club. There were two bands from neighboring high schools and a group of Scottish dancers with bagpipes from the city.

Karen was very pleased to see Charlotte Melville and two other contestants had been invited to ride in a convertible with a visiting television celebrity.

As they drove down the main street of Wilks, many people called out to Karen by name and she called back to them. She knew her voice was getting hoarse from all the shouting she was doing. Her feet hurt because of the high-heeled pink shoes. Her arms and shoulders were slightly sunburned by this time because the sun was overhead. She had a perpetual thirst from being without anything to drink for so long and she was beginning to develop a headache as well as being very hungry. Despite all of the physical discomforts that came with being queen, Karen still felt that the campaign and the contest were worth it. She felt especially good as they pulled in to the main intersection of town, where the temporary bleachers stood. There were two sets of bleachers that held about fifty people. They had been put up early in the morning for invited guests. Her mother and Lucy were sitting in them.

Karen's float slowed down to a very, very slow pace as they passed the bleachers. Karen was able to carry on a long, delightful conversation with her mother and Lucy about how successful the parade had been. Both her mother and Lucy looked ecstatic at seeing Karen up there on the float. They assured her that she looked breathtakingly lovely. Karen was pleased to see that her mother and Lucy looked lovely as well. Her mother was wearing a soft print dress that she had bought especially for the occasion. Her dark auburn hair with its slight speckles of gray looked extremely attractive because of the soft new haircut that Lucy had given her.

Beside her mother sat Tom Perkins. Since Tom seemed to be spending more time looking at Marsha Williams than at Karen, she felt more hopeful about her mother's possible romance than she ever had before.

Lucy was radiant in a peacock green sun dress with pink beads around her neck. Karen knew that her special beauty was because of her recent decision. Lucy was sitting beside her mother. There weren't any men around her but she did not seem to be unhappy about it.

Karen herself was feeling very good, though tired, and she was glad to see the end of the parade coming into view. It would be good to get off the bright blue moving platform and onto the solid earth again. She felt as though she had been sailing in a very rickety old boat for the last two months. Because the parade was so late, the hope for a nap was gone. But she was still looking forward to a late lunch and a few minutes' rest.

She had asked Roger to meet her at the bandstand at exactly six thirty. It was three-thirty right now. That meant that she was going to have to hurry if she was to get her shower and her rest and be back on time.

Even as she was stepping off the float platform onto the solid ground she was wondering if she had done the right thing by inviting Roger to meet her. She wanted desperately to try one more time to explain to Roger what had happened and why she had chosen to run for queen. But was tonight the night to do that? Was tonight the night to try to break through his prejudice about beauty contests and queens?

The questions revolved in Karen's head, but she knew that it had to be tonight or never. If there would ever be a time when she was going to be able to convince Roger that she had been correct in her decision to run for queen, this would be the night. She was feeling stronger and better about herself right now than she had ever felt before. Being queen made her feel powerful and in control of her life.

Tomorrow she would be Karen Williams again. She would no longer be Queen Karen. This was her magical day. Whatever she said to Roger, however she tried to explain things to him, she felt that this was her day. After all, she was the queen.

16

It was still light when Karen returned to the fairgrounds parking lot and began to look for Roger. She was not due to arrive at the fairgrounds until seven and that was why she had asked Roger to meet her at six thirty. It would give her thirty minutes to talk with him. Then she would sit on the platform and reign as queen for the Harvest Parade program.

Roger was waiting for her when she walked over to the bandstand. She was glad he was already there. It would have been more difficult for her to have to wait for him. When she saw him, she said, "Hi, Roger. I'm glad you're here."

He did not say that he was glad to be there. He only said, "Hi, Karen. Did you want to talk to me?"

"Yes. Yes, I did. I wanted to try to explain."

"You don't have to explain," Roger answered. "There's nothing to explain."

"Yes, there is," Karen said. "There are several things and I want very much for you to listen."

"Without interrupting?" Roger asked, his eyes twinkling.

"Please," Karen said. "Without interruption."

"Would you like to go sit somewhere?" Roger said. "I have the feeling this is going to be a very serious conversation."

"No. Standing up will be fine," Karen said quickly. Then she took a deep breath and began. "I know you don't really approve of Harvest Parades," she said.

"Oh, no," Roger said. "I approve of Harvest Parades."

"You promised not to interrupt," Karen reminded him gently.

"But I have to interrupt when you say that I don't approve of something that I *do* approve of," Roger said. "I approve of Harvest Parades. I think Harvest Parades are just fine and I think that people should participate in Harvest Parades if they want to. You missed the point, Karen, and I'd like to explain."

Karen shook her head. She smiled and said, "You promised me that I could talk first, Roger. This is really important to me. I want you to try and listen."

"Try and listen?" Roger asked. "I'm a good listener."

"Are you?" Karen rejoined quickly. "So far you're not doing a very good job."

That seemed to settle him down and Roger nodded silently and waited for Karen to continue.

She began again. "I know you don't approve of Harvest Parades and I know that you think that small towns are corny."

Again Roger looked as though he wanted to interrupt, but he pressed his lips firmly together and let Karen keep talking.

"When we talked that day," Karen said, "I was upset about running for the Harvest Queen. You told me I should drop out of the parade. I thought then that I wanted to. But after I thought about it, I decided that I didn't want to drop out. If I had dropped out of the parade I would have disappointed a lot of people."

Roger stopped her then. He said, "Karen, I'm not going to let you go on talking when about ninety percent of what you've said so far simply isn't true."

Karen's face flushed and she felt her heart begin to beat even more wildly. Her voice trembled as she answered Roger. "You promised me that you would listen. I'm trying the very best way I know how to explain myself to you. This is important to me. I can't go on letting you think the things that you think about me."

Roger shook his head stubbornly. "But that's just the point. You think I think a lot of things that aren't true. I can't let you go on thinking the things that you think about me. Won't you let me explain or try to explain to you one more time what it was that I was trying to say to you down by the river?"

"No!" Karen answered. "All the time I was riding in that parade I was thinking about how I was going to try to explain things to you! I was thinking that it was going to be my turn to talk. I listened to you down by the river and I just got confused by what you said. You're from the city and I'm from a small town. Sometimes we don't really understand each other. But I think we owe it to each other to listen. Now try and listen, Roger."

Roger's face seemed to close up on Karen even as she talked. She knew that he was not listening to her.

Tears welled in her eyes and her fists clenched. She wanted to grab him by the shoulders and shake him until she could make him pay attention to what she was saying. But she knew that she could never behave like that. Besides, it wouldn't do any good.

She spoke rapidly, trying again. "I know you don't think that what I did today was important. But it was important to my mother and it was important to my sister. Ever since I've been a little girl it's been something that people expected me to do. I am the Harvest Queen and I'm not going to apologize to you about that, Roger. I'm not going to tell you that I'm sorry I became the Harvest Queen."

Again Roger shook his head solemnly. He said, "Karen, I'm not going to stand here and listen to you talk like this. You're wrong. You think I disapprove of things and I don't. I know it's your day, and I know you're the queen. I know that sometimes people don't listen to you and I *have tried*. But you're going to have to listen to me now. I have some things I have to say to you. In the first place . . ." he began.

"There you are. They're waiting for you. You'll have to get on the platform right now. They're about to begin the program." It was Karen's mother and Lucy.

Karen looked helplessly at Roger and said, "Will you wait for me?"

Roger shrugged his shoulders and said, "It seems so pointless."

"Please wait," Karen said. "There has to be some way."

Roger did not answer her and Karen felt her heart sink as she turned with her mother and sister to walk up to the platform. She was sure that she had lost Roger forever. If only there had been a way to persuade Roger to stay! If only there had been a way to get

Roger to listen to her reasons and her arguments! She would have turned and run from her mother's and her sister's grasp and run back to Roger, but she was convinced now that it was hopeless.

There was nothing Karen could do except go through the formalities of the evening and try to put as good a face on things as she could. Pete and the other five young men were already on the platform when Karen got there. Pete reached over and held out his hand to Karen. He helped her walk up the rickety steps to get onto the platform. "Hi, Karen. Did you get some rest this afternoon?"

Karen nodded her head yes. She felt too numb to talk. She did manage to smile at Pete and the other escorts as she took her place at the center of the stage and waited for the president of the Chamber of Commerce to begin the program.

It was beginning to get dark now and the electric lights strung around the platform edges were turned on, attracting a lot of insects. Karen's mood changed from one of enthusiasm and optimism to one of grim determination. She would see the program through and behave in a way that was befitting a queen. Her movements were stiffer now. She was not as open-hearted and friendly as she had been earlier. Instead she moved with the tall, regal grace of a real queen. She found that it was easier to bow her head in acknowledgment to friends who were waving and calling to her than to be as bouncing and cheerful as she had been earlier.

She assumed Roger's refusal to listen to her was tantamount to a refusal of her altogether. She realized now that she had made a mistake in trying to talk to Roger during the contest. It had made it more difficult for her to enjoy her success. Nevertheless, she was fairly certain that no one else knew how upset she was. She prided herself on concealing her feelings because she did not want to spoil things for the others.

Her mother and Lucy were standing directly below the stage. Karen was gratified to see that Tom Perkins was still by her mother's side. There was no doubt in Karen's mind that Tom was interested in her mother and Karen was really very happy about that. Many emotions—so many feelings—raced through Karen's mind as she stood regally on the platform. No one out there would have been able to guess the depths of her feelings. During the hour that followed, she felt almost as though she were sleepwalking.

The president of the Chamber of Commerce talked on and on. Then it was the mayor's turn and, if anything, the mayor was longer than the president. After the mayor came the president of the Women's Club. After the president of the Women's Club talked for a long time, she introduced the high school principal. By the time the president of the Chamber of Commerce got around to calling on Karen for her speech, the people in the audience had been standing on one foot and then the other for forty-five minutes. Karen was glad that the evening dusk had at least brought some coolness to the landscape.

It was a warm evening, but not uncomfortably hot, and she was glad for that. She felt sure that if it had been too warm or too cold, she would have lost all of her audience except her mother and her sister.

Her mother and her sister and Pete all looked very proud as Karen went to the microphone to begin her speech. It pleased Karen that, even though Pete knew their romance was over, he was obviously enjoying her success. His face seemed unworried as he clapped for Karen as she walked to the front of the platform.

Karen's speech this evening was as simple and unpretentious as all of her speeches had been during the campaign. She went to great lengths to thank her mother and to thank her sister. She praised the town of Wilks, the people of Wilks. She praised the contest and the service clubs who put on the contest and then said something that was totally unprepared—something that she had not expected to say.

She said, "I would like to say that, although I won the contest, there were five other women who would have been very good queens. It is my hope that in the future those contestants who are not queen will be invited to ride in the lead float as attendants to the queen. It would have given me great pleasure to have Charlotte and the other contestants riding beside me. Although I enjoyed the handsome escorts, it seems to me that the girls deserve to be on the lead float also."

The audience's reception to her suggestion was very interesting. There were two or three sharp intakes of breath. People seemed for a minute not to understand that she was actually saying something different from what every queen had ever said before. Then, when they understood that her proposal was indeed a serious one, many of the people demonstrated their approval by a loud round of applause.

Karen was glad that her suggestion was received with as much enthusiasm as it had been. It made her hope that next year's contest would be run differently. She also hoped that Roger would know her suggestion demonstrated her accord with him. She felt good about her speech and she felt good about her suggestions. She felt even better when the program was over and she was able to rejoin Lucy and her mother.

Lucy gave her a great big hug and kiss and whispered

in her ear, "I think you were very brave to make the suggestion and you were dead right."

Her mother said nothing. She was obviously interested in talking with Tom Perkins. Pete and Tom both seemed determined to bring Cokes to the women as quickly as their legs could carry them back and forth to the refreshment stands.

Karen ate supper with Lucy, her mother, Tom, and Pete. For supper they had the usual Harvest Parade fare. Her appetite was as huge as it had been at the first barbecue. Karen loaded her plate just as heavily as before. There were wonderful garden vegetables and juicy red ripe tomatoes to put on the green salads.

For dessert there was pecan pie. Karen ate two slices, laughing as they teased her, saying it was a good thing she didn't plan to wear the pink dress again soon because it had been a lot of trouble to slip her into it that morning. "From now on," her sister said, "it will be impossible."

Karen assured everyone that she intended to go on a diet next week, but that this was her night to celebrate. To the dismay of everyone at the table, she ate a piece of apple pie after finishing the two pieces of pecan pie.

By the time they finished eating, it was quite dark. The parking lot had taken on a certain magical atmosphere. Over in one corner there was a small children's merry-go-round, as well as two or or three other small kiddie-car rides.

The only ride that was really suitable for adults was the Ferris wheel. Pete teased Karen by saying, "I wouldn't dare take the Queen of the Harvest Parade on that."

"Especially after three pieces of pie," Lucy reminded them both. Karen had to admit that her stomach was feeling queasy enough so that it probably wasn't a good idea.

They sat and talked for a while. The conversation was very light. Indeed, there would not have been any way to engage in a serious conversation because every few minutes people came up to congratulate Karen on her success. Karen had to drop her conversation with her immediate family and chat for a while with the visitors who came to the table.

She was beginning to feel relief that the day was almost over. Though her mother kept reminding her that this was the best day of her life, Karen felt that wasn't true. She would have many other wonderful days, she promised herself.

Looking through the crowd for Roger got to be impossible because it was too dark. Roger would not be coming back. She had to accept the inevitable. She had lost Roger, though she had won the contest. She told herself again, there was never a happiness without sadness. She determined to dedicate her evening to making other people happy. When Sue came by to congratulate her, Karen was friendly. Whatever Sue's problems were, she would have to work them out on her own. The loss of Sue did not seem as difficult to accept as it once had. She had had time to get used to the idea.

It was the loss of Roger that Karen was finding so very difficult to accept. Only two hours ago she was hoping she would find some way to get through to Roger. Now that hope had closed for her forever.

Her sister Lucy leaned over the table and whispered, "Smile. This is your lucky day."

Karen looked up at her sister, batted back the tears that were gathering in her eyes, smiled, and said,

"You're right. I think I'll take a walk before the dance starts."

Pete stood up and said, "I'll go with you."

Karen looked at Pete, shook her head sadly, and said, "Pete, I'd rather go alone."

Pete frowned. "You're not going to disappear on us, are you?"

She reached up, touched Pete's arm, and smiled again in what she hoped was a reassuring manner. She said, "I promise I won't disappear. I'll be here till the end of the dance. It's just that I ate too much pie. I want to walk it off."

Pete shook his head and said, "You never ate too much pie in your life. No. You're sad, Karen. I hate to see you sad."

Karen could think of nothing to say to that except, "Thank you." She left Pete and began aimlessly walking through the crowd across the parking lot. She wanted to be by herself for a few seconds, to think things out, so that she could face the evening with a cheerful smile.

Because she had on the long pink dress, she was clearly visible as the queen. As she moved through the crowd, people stopped her, said hello, and congratulated her. One or two people insisted on chatting with her for a long time.

Karen was amused when Mrs. Persip, the little neighbor lady who had such a nosy interest in her family, stopped her and insisted that she and both her sisters had voted for Karen after all. Karen graciously thanked the little old lady, even though she was sure it was not really true. She continued walking until she was on the outskirts of the crowd and over on the side of the shopping mall where the floats were parked.

She walked to the Lions Club float that she had

ridden and pulled one of the pink crepe paper flowers from the side of the float. As she pulled the flower away from the float, a deep male voice asked, "Hey, lady, what you doin'?"

Karen turned around, ready to explain that she only wanted a souvenir of the evening, then realized that the voice was Roger's.

Roger was standing directly behind her. There was a streetlight about fifty yards behind him; the light streamed down onto his face. It had the same mysterious quality that moonlight had. It seemed to light up Roger's face, making him look older, sadder, and more mature than Karen had ever seen him look before. That's the way he'll look when he's forty, Karen thought to herself.

She reached forward, holding the flower in her two hands, and said in a quiet voice, "I was going to pin it on the wall in my room. It's a souvenir."

Roger pulled another crepe paper flower off the side of the float and handed it to her, saying, "Here, take two. They're free." Then he smiled at her and asked, "Are you ready to listen to me yet?"

Karen opened her mouth to protest that it was he who hadn't listened. But then she closed her mouth and nodded, saying, "I'll try."

Roger nodded his head up and down and began talking. He spoke in a low, deep, serious voice, and he had not gone very far before Karen realized that what he was telling her were things he probably hadn't told anyone before.

He began by saying, "You know I have a brother in medical school. What you don't know is that I used to have a sister as well. My sister's name was Karen also." Then he smiled and shook his head quickly. "No, you don't remind me of her at all. She didn't look a thing like you and she wasn't anything like you. But you have the same name and you have something of the same problem. Or at least when I first met you I thought that you and my sister Karen might have more in common than I wanted to know. You see, my sister Karen had a medical problem that she couldn't get over. She'd been in a car accident when she was in her early teens and had crippled one leg. Though she was a very pretty girl, she walked with a limp. She was afraid that people would look at her as different—that they wouldn't want her as a friend. To make a long story short, Karen was a girl who liked to have friends. She liked to please people the way you like to please people. In order to be popular she got into drugs and she ended up killing herself. So you see, now you know the real reason why my family moved to Wilks and left the big city. It had to do with Karen's death."

Karen reached out her hand and took Roger's in her hands as she said, "I'm so sorry. I had no idea."

"No, of course not," Roger said, "because, you see, it's a secret. It's a thing we don't talk about."

"I'll never tell anyone," Karen assured him.

Roger shook his head and smiled and said, "I never thought you would," he said gently. "I only told you because I wanted to explain what it was I was saying that day by the river. I was trying to tell you it's very important not to need people so much that you'll do anything to please them. Never give up on those things that you really want for yourself. It isn't that I was against the contest, Karen—though I admit I never expected to fall in love with a beauty queen. The only reason I was against the contest was because you seemed so unhappy. And you're wrong if you think I think Wilks is a corny little town. I think Wilks is a wonderful place to live. That's why we moved here—

because it is a wonderful place to live. It's good to have clean air and birds and the wholesome, simple things of life."

But Karen wasn't really listening as Roger talked. She had heard the one thing that Roger said that seemed most important to her.

She let him talk some more about the virtues of Wilks, Kansas, and then she asked, "Roger, did you really mean it?"

He looked at her quizzically, "Mean it? Of course I mean it! Do you think I'd tell you these things if I didn't mean it?"

"No, no. I know you meant it about your sister and about Wilks, but did you mean the other part—the part about being in love with a beauty queen?"

Roger's face clouded. He nodded. "Yes, Karen. I am in love with you, but I realize that to you I'm just an outsider and you could never be interested in me. It's all right. Pete's a nice person. I can see why Pete is your choice."

"But he isn't," Karen said. She lifted her arms to put her hands on his shoulders. She stepped closer to him, into the ring of magical light. She whispered, "Roger, you just don't understand anything, do you? I've been trying to tell you ever since that day at the bridge that Pete isn't my choice. You are my choice. You are my very own wonderful choice."

With that, she reached up on tiptoe and kissed Roger. He seemed startled for a moment and did not respond to her kiss. Then, as the knowledge that Karen meant what she was saying seemed to sink into his consciousness, he put his arms around her and drew her close to him and pressed his lips against hers.

The kiss seemed to go on and on, as though time had stopped in their magical world. Karen was conscious enough to notice that her response to Roger's embrace was every bit as strong as it had been the first time he kissed her.

She had no idea how much time had passed before Roger drew back, looked down at her, and laughed softly as he said, "Now it's your turn."

"My turn?" Karen said. "I'm the one who made the advances both times we've kissed."

Roger laughed. "No, no. I meant now it's your turn to talk."

Suddenly Karen remembered that she had been trying to explain her position to him. Now it did not seem important. The most important thing in the world seemed to be the fact that Roger was interested in her after all.

She began rapidly, not wanting to waste too much of the precious evening. "I thought you weren't interested in me," Karen said. "I thought you thought—I thought you thought . . ." and then her voice trailed off and she began again. "The point is, I never wanted to be the queen of the parade. Ever since I was a little girl, people told me that I would want to be, but I didn't. You helped me see that, but by then it was too late. My mother and my sister would have been so disappointed. I love my mother and I love my sister and I want to see them happy. You see, I know that I was trying to please them, but I was also trying to make them happy. That didn't seem like such a terrible thing to me. Does it to you, Roger?"

She waited for his response.

He wrinkled his brow and seemed to think it over. Finally he said, "Karen, I'm sure you did what you thought was right. If you thought it was right, then that's all that's important."

"But you would have dropped from the contest?" Karen asked.

At that Roger laughed and shook his head. Then he wagged his finger in front of her nose and said, "You still haven't learned, have you? It isn't important what I would have done. What's important is that *you* did what *you* think is right. Besides that, they never would have elected me. I'm kind of pretty, but I'm from out of town."

Karen laughed loudly at the idea of Roger running for queen and said, "I don't think you're as pretty as Charlotte Melville anyway."

He said, "Gee, that's funny. I think you're every bit as pretty as Charlotte or any of the other girls there." Then his face changed and he said, "Seriously, Karen, all I want is for you to be happy. If being queen of the contest made you happy, then I'm happy. And now we've got to talk about our future."

"Our future," Karen said, and suddenly her future seemed to be full of promise. She was able to joke about her future for the first time in a long, long time.

She said, "Well, the first thing in our future is for you to give me another kiss. Then we must go back to the parking lot and dance. We must dance every dance we can possibly dance, except I should warn you, everyone else is going to ask me to dance as well as you."

"Does that mean," Roger asked, "that I'm going to be a wallflower?"

"Of course not," Karen said. "You will probably ask Charlotte and Janet and all of the other contestants to dance."

Roger wrinkled his nose and said, "So you're foisting me off on the losers."

Karen laughed and answered, "Losers, winners—

what does it mean? After tonight none of it is going to matter. It will be all over in three more hours."

"But the evening has just begun," Roger said. "You and I are going to enjoy it as much as we can."

"Good," Karen said. "I'm glad that we agree on that." She squeezed his hand and said, "Now we'd better go back to the dance. They'll be worried about me."

"Not quite yet," Roger said. "Remember, you promised me a kiss."

If you enjoyed this book...

...you will enjoy a *First Love* from Silhouette subscription even more. It will bring you each new title, as soon as it is published every month, delivered right to your door.

Filled with the challenges, excitement and anticipation that make first love oh, so wonderful, *First Love* romances are new and different. Every *First Love* romance is an original novel—never before published—and all written by leading authors.

If you enjoyed this book, treat yourself, or some friend, to a one-year subscription to these romantic originals. We'll ship two NEW $1.75 romances each month, a total of 24 books a year. So send in your coupon now. **There's nothing quite as special as a First Love.**

First Love from Silhouette

THERE'S NOTHING QUITE AS SPECIAL AS A <u>FIRST LOVE</u>.

$1.75 each

_____ #1 NEW BOY IN TOWN, Dorothy Francis

_____ #2 GIRL IN THE ROUGH, Josephine Wunsch

_____ #3 PLEASE LET ME IN, Patti Beckman

_____ #4 SERENADE, Adrienne Marceau

_____ #5 FLOWERS FOR LISA, Veronica Ladd

_____ #6 KATE HERSELF, Helen Erskine

_____ #7 SONGBIRD, Carrie Enfield

_____ #8 SPECIAL GIRL, Dorothy Francis

_____ #9 LOVE AT FIRST SIGHT, Elaine Harper

_____ #10 PLEASE LOVE ME...SOMEBODY, Maud Johnson

_____ #11 IT'S MY TURN, Eleni Carr

_____ #12 IN MY SISTER'S SHADOW, Genell Dellin

_____ #13 SOMETIME MY LOVE, Oneta Ryan

_____ #14 PROMISED KISS, Veronica Ladd

FIRST LOVE, Department FL/4
1230 Avenue of the Americas
New York, NY 10020

Please send me the books I have checked above. I am enclosing $_____ (please add 50¢ to cover postage and handling. NYS and NYC residents please add appropriate sales tax). Send check or money order—no cash or C.O.D.'s please. Allow six weeks for delivery.

NAME_____

ADDRESS_____

CITY_____ STATE/ZIP_____

6 brand new Silhouette Romance novels yours for 15 days—Free!

If you enjoyed this Silhouette First Love, and would like to move on to even more thrilling, satisfying stories then Silhouette Romances are for you. Enjoy the challenges, conflicts, and joys of love. Sensitive heroines will enchant you—powerful heroes will delight you as they sweep you off to adventures around the world.

6 Silhouette Romances, free for 15 days!

We'll send you 6 new Silhouette Romances to keep for 15 days, absolutely free! If you decide not to keep them, send them back to us. You pay nothing.

FREE HOME DELIVERY. But if you enjoy them as much as we think you will, keep them by paying the invoice enclosed with your free trial shipment. You'll then automatically become a member of the Silhouette Book Club and receive 6 more new Silhouette romances every month.

There is no minimum number of books to buy and you can cancel at any time.